UNFRIENDLY RELATIONS

SADIE HALLER

QTP

ABOUT THIS BOOK

Looking to hook up with a potentially compatible kinky fellow aristocrat near you? There's an app for that.

I'd imagined my wedding day countless times as a young girl, complete with Prince Charming.

True, there is a prince. But charming? Not even close.

DISCLAIMER

Using a badly forged artistic license, I've taken inexcusable liberties with the long and storied British monarchy. This is not your great-auntie Dot's royal family.

PROLOGUE

Duncan

"Did you have to be seen, and photographed, in public with that slut?"

And here we go. I knew this was coming.

"She was a victim, Mum. She didn't do anything wrong, and she's suffered more than enough, thanks to that asshole producer."

"You could have at least brought in Frobisher and had those photos blocked from publication."

"But why should I?"

"For the sake of your family?"

As always, I—the youngest in a long line of sons—am the one shouldering all the blame for the Royal Family's unpopularity. "Not a good enough reason for me to throw a friend under the bus. Those photos helped to restore a little of her reputation. And given the way she'd been snubbed by so many she'd considered friends? I was more than happy to do what little I could."

"Yes, yes, that's very noble, but—"

"No buts. It's done. I'd do it again. Good talk."

And with that, I leave.

Charlotte

I don't know what I was thinking, going to a BDSM club and then going home with a stranger. I got out, but not before he hurt me, humiliated me, and took compromising photos.

At least I had the presence of mind to call Winston Frobisher as soon as I left and realised I was in deep trouble.

Funny, when I left school, I never thought I'd be one of *those girls*, the ones everyone knew would need his help. Fortunately, Matron made sure we all had the contact information for the fixer to the snobs, not just the girls who were obviously going to find themselves in sticky situations.

"Charlotte, you're going to have to give me the details. I can't make this go completely away if I don't know exactly what I'm dealing with."

He's surprisingly gentle. Careful.

But no matter how sweet and caring he comes across, he's still a man, and there's no way I can tell my stupid, humiliating story to a man. "I want to, but it's too embarrassing. Shameful. I just can't—"

"Would you be able to talk to a woman? One I trust completely?"

Would I? I need to tell someone if I'm going to have any chance of coming out of this unscathed.

"I think so."

He pats my shoulder gently. "All right, then. I'll bring you up a nice cup of tea."

"Thank you."

"It'll be fine. I'll make sure of it. I promise."

He comes back a few minutes later with a hot mug of tea and a plate of scones slathered in clotted cream and jam.

"There you go, love. Mel will be here soon, and we'll get this mess sorted."

"Thank you."

My stomach is in knots, but I can't resist taking a bite of scone. Which leads me to another and another, until it's gone and I'm feeling a little bit better. I take a long sip of my tea and sigh. Some cups of tea are exactly right. The right strength, the right amount of milk, and the right temperature. This is that cup.

By the time Winston knocks on my door, announcing the arrival of the mysterious Mel, I'm much calmer.

"Lady Charlotte, I'm Mel Seymour, and Winston tells me you've had a bit of a rough night."

"Please, just call me Charlotte. I don't really go for that title business."

"Charlotte, then. How about you tell me everything that happened, so we can get this all taken care of."

ONE

Duncan

"Just, please tell me you're not going to do anything that will put you on the front page of the tabloids," my twin sister, Alexandra pleads from the other end of the phone.

"I won't. But only because you're asking me so nicely."

"Duncan, be serious. You're walking a dreadfully thin line these days. I think the royal 'rents are just about ready to cut you loose."

"Let them. I'd welcome it, truly. I'm really just excess baggage. They've got heirs and spares aplenty."

"They love you. We all do, but honestly, sometimes you go too far."

"Xandra, I promise. I will be a good boy tonight. It's been a stressful week, and I'm just going out to Scaffold to have a few drinks and let off some steam."

"I'm holding you to it because it's always me

everyone comes to after your ugly mug gets plastered all over the tabloids and gossip sites. I swear, there should be hazard pay or something for being your twin."

I smile. She loves me, really. And as far as I'm concerned, the sun rises and sets on her. "Nobody will be complaining to you. Have a good night doing...what are you doing tonight, anyway?"

"It's book club."

I try not to laugh outright. All I care about is her happiness, and if hanging around with a bunch of frumpy-dumps discussing highbrow literature is her jam, I am perfectly fine with that.

"Have fun at your book club, baby sister."

As expected, she growls her displeasure.

"You know, if we'd been born in any normal family, nobody would have cared which one of us came two minutes ahead of the other. And really, by the time you get to the fifth and sixth kid, royal or not, does it really matter?"

"It does to me." I poke again. It's been a bone of contention with her as far back as I can remember. I can absolutely see her point, though. We were born by caesarean, and it was entirely luck of the draw which of us they yanked out first.

"Good night, Xandra. I love you."

"Love you too, jerk."

I wait until she disconnects the call, like I always do. I never want my sister to feel like I've cut her off.

"Craig, are you nearly ready to go?" I call out to my

bodyguard as I slip my phone into my front trouser pocket.

"Whenever you are."

He gives me a long-suffering look that conveys precisely how much he'd really prefer I stay home tonight. And I'll admit, it's actually tempting. At thirty-four, I'm starting to feel a little old for the party-boy life, but I've cultivated a reputation that, for some inexplicable reason, I feel the need to maintain.

Besides, I'm feeling an itch for some action. It's been a few weeks since I've hooked up with anyone—something I truly think Craig should be grateful for. The mad panic background checks he needs to arrange whenever I hookup with someone new drive him mad. I keep telling him that he doesn't need to. That there shouldn't be anyone with access to the app who could pose a problem for me. But Craig has been my man for so many years—he simply does not take chances with my safety.

"We're going to Scaffold," I tell him. "You know the deal."

"Private access, beefy security, and a tight rein on who gets in. I guess if you insist on going out tonight, there is no shortage of worse security disasters you could have picked."

As much as we both bitch about my social life—me, over how restricted I feel, and him over how reckless I am —I do try to be mindful of the position I put him in when I decide where I want to go out. He's got a difficult job, and while I don't like to be too constrained in my entertainment options, it would be exceptionally shitty of me to completely disregard the burden I am on him.

"I'll try not to make it too late a night, okay?"

He chuckles. "Translation—you plan on bringing home a play-date."

"You never know—maybe we'll get lucky and I'll bring home someone who needs more than I'm equipped to provide on my own."

TWO

Charlotte

Some days, I wonder why I bother. Then I look out the window and into the paddock at the rag-tag herd of rescued beasties we provide sanctuary for. Rehoming can be difficult, but rarely impossible. It just tends to take a lot of time for the right fit to come along.

Unfortunately, raising the necessary funds to care for these poor creatures is not easy, and no matter how hard I pinch the pennies, there is never quite enough money coming in to cover what must go out.

And my personal inventory of valuables worth selling continues to shrink at an alarming rate.

Still, if I had it all to do over again, I wouldn't change a thing.

Kevin, my three-legged border collie, rubs his head against my leg, and I absently reach down to stroke his silky head.

"Time to go pester the girls, is it?" I ask him. The stub of his tail wiggles at a ridiculous rate.

I can only piece together his story based on his injuries and the state he was in when I found him, but the trauma my boy has suffered in his past makes me want to commit unspeakable acts of violence.

He's one of the reasons I do what I do. So many animals are thrown away when they reach the end of their perceived usefulness.

Kevin handles sheep just as well as any other herding dog. In fact, I'd argue he's better than most.

"Come on then, my good boy, let's go."

At the back door, I slide my feet into my wellies and pop on a jacket before heading out to the sheep paddock.

Currently, we've got seventy-eight rescued ewes and a geriatric ram. The old boy tries his best, but this isn't a breeding program, so we leave them to do as they please. Well, except when I'm working with the dogs.

Kevin doesn't really require the training anymore, but as a working dog, he needs to keep his paw in, so to speak, to maintain both his physical and mental well-being.

We've got three other rescued herding dogs at the moment. While there are breed-specific rescues, we take on the ones that are harder to find forever homes for. We're under less pressure to move them on, and as a result, there is less risk of a return when they finally do get a new situation.

I work with Kevin for about half an hour with roughly a quarter of the herd, and then I take him to the barn to hang out with Maisie, my Shire-Thoroughbred cross. They love each other to bits, and Kevin is much happier to hang out with my mare while I work the other dogs than he is alone in my office.

Actually, *I'm* happier when he's not alone in my office, because even when he's been worked hard, he still manages to find himself some mischief, bless him.

It takes me a little more than an hour to work the other dogs. I have hopes to be able to start working them in teams, but their social skills are still lacking.

Once I've returned the last dog to her kennel, I go to Maisie's stall and give her a thorough grooming. I'd love to go for a ride this afternoon, but I must be off to the city as soon as I'm done here for the day.

I have back-to-back meetings tomorrow, so I've decided I deserve to avail myself of some nightlife before I must sit through a bevy of insufferable blowhards.

Thankfully, we have an amazing crew of volunteers, including a number who don't mind being here on nights I can't.

Once the car is packed, and I'm ready to go, I take Kevin to the staff room.

"You're going to be a good boy for Darren, aren't you, my love?"

I know he won't. He's only ever decently behaved for me. But Darren loves the cheeky boy almost as much as I do.

"He'll be just fine, Lady Charlotte."

It doesn't matter how hard I try to get Darren to be

less formal, he insists upon using my title. I've all but given up, now. But somehow it rankles. Like it sets me apart, when really, I just want to be on an equal footing. A colleague.

"Thank you, Darren. I really do appreciate you holding down the fort like this."

"Happy to help. And it's always a joy to hang out with Kevin. We like having our boy's nights."

"Well, have fun, you two. I'm due back tomorrow evening."

I hate not bringing Kevin along. But sometimes I don't have a choice. It's kinder to leave him here where he can have free run of the place and the love of people instead of being stuck alone in my flat for hours on end. And getting himself into trouble.

Normally, I would take the train into the city, but on top of the meetings tomorrow, I've been asked by one of my cousins to come and assess a pony he's considering for his daughter.

My veterinary practice is pretty much constrained to the sanctuary, however, I do occasionally provide services to friends, acquaintances, and a select few family members, like my cousin, Alfred.

It's nearly eight when I arrive at my London flat, and I'm starving. I run to the little chip shop around the corner and grab a sausage and chips.

Not even close to healthy, and I'm sure there are those in the world who are convinced I should be a committed vegan, given my deep love of animals. And in truth, there are some meats I can happily live without.

Lamb, for instance, but there is no way I could give up chippy sausages.

I'm just about finished eating when a text comes in.

TILDA: I'm so sorry, something came up and I can't make it tonight.

Charlotte: No worries, babes. Next time.

THREE

Duncan

Scaffold is absolutely heaving when we arrive, and I don't need to look at Craig to know how unhappy he is about it.

I suppose it will have to be a quick drink while I score my evening's entertainment, and then we'll go.

According to my Fetwrk app, there are fifteen possible matches waiting for me when I enter Scaffold, one of the most exclusive clubs in London. The place to see and be seen. And much to the chagrin of my parents, I'm all about being seen.

I scroll through the evening's offerings, hoping someone will catch my eye. I've come to a point in my life where I'm pretty jaded. I rarely hook up with the same person twice if I can help it, because I'm not looking to settle down, and I don't want anyone to interpret a couple of kinky fucks as a proposal of marriage and a position, however lowly, in the royal family.

I stop scrolling when I come across Cock-Doc. Also known as Lady Charlotte Grey, veterinarian and animal philanthropist. She's one of the very few women I've hooked up with more than two or three times for a number of reasons, not the least of which is she's a tremendously great fuck. She's always down for every filthy, kinky thing I can concoct. And I know for a fact she has zero interest in elevating her social status.

Yeah, she'll be perfect tonight.

I swipe on her profile, letting her know I'm interested as I watch her from my spot not far from the bar. And I'm mildly annoyed she doesn't immediately accept. I scan the crowded room, wondering who on earth could be here that she would consider to be a better bet for the night than me?

FOUR

Charlotte

The minute I walk into the club, my mobile starts sending me notifications. God, I love this app. No more risky encounters that force me to turn to Winston Frobisher.

As lovely as he is, one rescue was more than enough to keep me on the relatively straight and narrow.

I flick through my notifications, most of which are instant rejects.

Then I stop short.

Ugh. Prince fucking Duncan and his massive ego. I consider the two other guys I've swiped up to my short-list, but gargantuan ego aside, Duncan is an excellent Dom, kinky as fuck, and always generous with the orgasms.

And just like that, I opt for the devil I know and an evening of guaranteed happy endings.

"Charlotte," he croons in my ear as he sidles up to me barely a minute later. "Shall we go?" He means to his place. Which I'm perfectly happy with because I'm exceptional at not wearing out my welcome.

We leave through the VIP exit, where his car is waiting.

His bodyguard, Craig, never ceases to impress me with how unobtrusive he is. And not for the first time, I wonder if he's ever done a threesome with Duncan. I dismiss the idea as ridiculous. But he's sexy as fuck, and what girl wouldn't want to be the filling in a prince and pauper sandwich?

Not me, as it turns out. The concept is sexy, but I don't think I would be comfortable with it as a real-life experience.

Once we're all safely inside Duncan's apartment, Craig disappears, leaving us to get our kink on in private.

"Do you need water before we get started?" Duncan asks.

"No, thank you."

"Then go make use of the facilities. As you know, I prefer not to have a scene interrupted if it can be avoided."

"Yes, Sir." I've always found it interesting that when he's dominating me, his ego takes a backseat. As a prince, it's reasonable for him to expect me to call him Your Highness, yet he opts for Sir.

When I'm done in the loo, he escorts me to his playroom.

God, if the paparazzi ever got a look inside here...

FIVE

Charlotte

"Strip." Duncan's order sends a shiver through me just like it always does. It's a good kind of shiver, one that no other Dom has been able to elicit.

We both know from prior experience that he expects me to fold my clothes neatly and leave them on the small bench near the door.

As soon as soon as I'm naked, I stand and wait for further instructions.

"So, Charlotte, have you been a good girl since we last played?"

"Of course, Sir. I'm always a good girl."

He smiles at me. It's a deliciously dastardly smile. The only thing missing is one of those long, thin moustaches for him to twirl around his fingers, like those villains in old black and white films.

Yes, I was the girl who wanted to be tied up by that

villain, and fucked rough and hard, not rescued by the goody-two-shoes hero who's probably super-polite during sex. *"Would you mind so terribly if I were to slide my tab A into your slot B, my dear?"*

I'm all for consent, but that kind of bollocks would send me batshit crazy for sure.

"Charlotte?"

"Yes, Sir."

"If you're bored..." he trails off, angling his head toward the door.

"No, I'm sorry, Sir."

"Facing the cross, then, love."

I hurry to the other side of the room and spread my arms and legs. Moments later, Duncan joins me, fastening my wrists and ankles to the cross.

"I'm feeling a bit mean tonight, Charlotte. Are you up for mean?"

"Yes please, Sir." I need to let go, and Duncan is very good at taking me completely out of my head. If he wasn't such an asshole outside of a scene, it's possible I could fall for him.

But there is no future in a relationship based solely on kinky sex—even if it's stellar kinky sex. Fortunately, for now anyway, I'm only interested in some very stellar kinky sex. Because really, if I could tie myself up and spank my own ass, I'm fairly sure I wouldn't need a man for anything.

His warm hand slides over my ass, making me squirm in anticipation. The first strike is feather light. More of a brush off than a smack. Almost an annoyance. He did say he was feeling mean, so he's going to make me suffer in the most terrible ways he can think of. Sometimes that suffering is pain, other times, it's frustration.

"Charlotte, I want to leave marks tonight. Marks that will remind you of me for many days. Some of which will remind you every time you sit down. Do I have your permission?

"None that will show and raise questions?"

"Provided you don't go about in public wearing nothing but a thong bikini, they'll be just between us. And, of course, anyone else you hook up with between tonight and when they fade into oblivion."

He's claiming territory, but I don't give a flying fuck. Considering the social lives we lead, it would be completely unreasonable for a Dom to hook up with a sub and expect her to be clear of any other Dom's marks.

In fact, there's a small part of me that would love to force Duncan to face another Dom's marks on me. It's never happened because I don't hook up to play often enough for there to still be marks from one Dom to the next.

"Then I'm good with marks, Sir."

I watch him from the corner of my eye while he roots through a drawer in the cabinet along the wall to my left. He comes back with a thin stick about a foot long and stands to the side.

"Hold yourself away from the cross until just the very tips of your nipples are touching the surface."

As soon as I'm in position, he pulls back on the tip of the stick, and lets it fly against my nipple. It takes a second or two for the pain to register and the scream to escape.

"I told you I was feeling mean tonight," he says as he moves to my right side. This time I flinch because I know exactly what I'm in for. "Oh dear, Charlotte. You know better than to move. That's how injuries happen. That's also how you get extra strokes. Now be a good girl and remain still until I'm done."

I shut my eyes this time, thinking it might be better if I don't know when it's coming. I scream again as the pain registers. I also learn that it's almost worse not knowing when it's coming.

He lets the tip fly against my right nipple again, before returning to my left. I'm still reeling from the ouch, when I'm vaguely aware of him crouched between my legs.

Oh. Fuck.

"No—please, Sir. I can't take that. I just can't."

"What is your safeword, Charlotte?"

"Red, Sir."

"Are you tapping out?"

I think on that for a second. "No, Sir."

"Then I suggest you say nothing at all, unless it's your safeword."

The pain to my clit goes well beyond that which my nipples just endured. I'm grateful he only forbade me to talk, because there was no way I could have held back the screams. Not from that first strike, or the three that follow.

I'm panting hard when Duncan whispers in my ear.

"There's a reason they call that an evil stick, love. And I promise, you've not seen the last of it tonight. But right now, I'm going to fuck you. How do you want it?"

"Rough. Hard and rough, please, Sir."

"It will be my pleasure."

The tell-tale jangle of his belt, the slide of his zip and the crinkle of a condom wrapper are all the warning I get before he drives into me, forcing me hard against the wood of the cross, and rekindling the fire in my nipples.

He reaches around and plays with my clit as he slams into me—hard, fast, and completely without mercy.

"Come for me right now, Charlotte," he demands as his fingers press and rub and slide over my clit until I have no choice but to obey him. As if that's an order I would ever consider defying.

As my orgasm takes over, Duncan's thrusts become more punishing. He pounds me into the cross with a force sure to leave bruises. He continues fucking me long after the last spasm of my orgasm is gone. "You'd better come at least once more, love. If you can still walk and think by the time I'm done with you, I won't be satisfied."

His fingers worry at my clit again, and I shouldn't have been surprised at the speed with which he makes me come again.

"Such a good girl for me. Now it's my turn." He slides his hands up my body and cups my breasts. He pinches my nipples hard, making me scream. Seconds later, he lets out a long, low groan in my ear as he comes deep inside my body.

He unfastens me from the cross, carries me to his bedroom, and lays me gently on the bed.

"I've gone hard on you tonight, and you've been such a good girl, taking it all for me." He traces the tip of his finger over the welts on my nipples. "So pretty. How are you feeling?"

"Good."

"Do you think you're up for more?"

"Yes, please."

"On your belly."

I flip over and he traces the welts on my backside. "Seeing my marks on you makes me hard. Ass up, knees under you and spread. Wide."

As soon as I do, his mouth is on my pussy. His tongue spears its way inside me as his upper lip rubs against my sore clit. His tongue is replaced with two fingers and he fucks me hard while he sucks my clit. "Come for me, Charlotte. I want it all." His voice resonates against my most sensitive parts and my world explodes. He doesn't stop until he's wrung out every last tremor of my orgasm.

"Rest, love. I'm going to use you hard again soon."

Much, much later, Duncan's breathing transitions to the slow steady rhythm of sleep. I wait a little longer, until I'm sure he's deep enough for me to make my getaway undetected.

I slip into his *en suite* and allow myself a quick peek at the marks he's left. After a short rest from round one, he'd decided the only proper way to leave clear, lasting marks was to give me a good, hard caning. From the top of my ass down to mid-thigh. No short skirts for me for a while—though to be fair, he did ask permission to go that far beforehand. My breasts are all marked up too. Bites, cane stripes, more evil stick to my nipples.

Yes, tonight will be uppermost in my mind for quite some time.

Of course, Craig is in the lounge when I emerge with my shoes, coat, and bag in hand.

"I'm sorry to have kept you up so late." My voice is hoarse. But that's hardly surprising, given how much more Duncan made me scream tonight.

"You didn't. There's a car waiting out front to take you home."

"You didn't need to do that, you know."

He just smiles as he escorts me out to the hallway. "Good night, Lady Charlotte," he says as the door closes and locks behind me.

We've had this same exchange a number of times now. It's almost like something would be dreadfully wrong if we didn't.

As promised, when I exit the building, there's a car to take me back to my own flat. I could walk. But I suppose Craig doesn't want to risk blow-back on the prince if, for some reason, I didn't make it safely back home.

SIX

Duncan

The next morning, I'm woken by Craig knocking on my bedroom door.

As she's done every other time we've hooked up, Charlotte has vacated my bed while I slept. This shouldn't annoy me, but it does. Any other woman, and I'd be relieved.

"Sorry to bother you, but considering you've not responded to numerous calls and texts, I've been tasked with informing you that you're expected this evening at seven."

"Thank you, Craig."

No need to ask where or by whom. I'm just surprised it's taken this long for my parents to summon me for yet another royal reprimand.

When I walk into the family salon at precisely ten-past-seven, I'm confronted by my four older brothers and their spouses in addition to my parents.

Clearly, they're going for maximum humiliation.

Fuck.

"Duncan." My mother makes a point of looking at her wristwatch. My father may be king, but when it comes to the family, there is no question my mother is in charge. "So lovely of you to find a way to squeeze us in somewhere between your hedonism and debauchery. Do have a seat." She gestures toward the only unoccupied chair in the room, and I drop into it, adopting the most careless attitude I can muster while I have ten pairs of eyes glaring at me.

"I'll get directly to the point," my mother says. "Your behaviour is becoming increasingly outrageous, and it simply must stop. Our family is already struggling with public opinion. Your antics are only pushing us farther and farther out of favour."

"I didn't ask to be born into this family. I'm the fifth son of the reigning monarch. I do not feed off the public tit, nor do I exploit my pedigree. I pay taxes, I pay my bills, and purchase my own belongings. In every way that's meaningful, I am no different than any other person in this country."

"Regardless of how you live your life in reality, that is not the public's perception. They see you as nothing more than a spoilt playboy prince."

"So what? Again, I am an independent person. I owe the public nothing."

"But you do, at the very least, owe your *family* some

loyalty. We've put up with your shenanigans for entirely too long. It's time for you to settle down and prove yourself responsible and respectable. How do you think the public will treat your nieces and nephews when they're older if you continue in this direction?"

"My behaviour keeps the tabloids too busy to bother with the children. And when they do get to an age where they're more in the spotlight—I'm a cautionary tale."

"Duncan, you are most certainly a cautionary tale. In fact, you've risen well above and beyond that. Now, it's time you turn your life around. Build a shiny new reputation. One you can be proud of."

"Mother, yet again, I am self-sufficient and successful, which is something I am inordinately proud of. What you're really telling me is to build a shiny new reputation *you* can be proud of."

"If you won't listen to reason, then you give us no alternative. If you are not engaged to a *suitable* woman within six months from today, access to your nieces and nephews will be withheld until such time as you *are* engaged to a suitable woman, whom you will marry within a year."

"That is not fair to the children."

"No, it's not. So it is entirely up to you to ensure the children don't miss out on spending time with their favourite uncle, now, isn't it?"

I have to give them credit. They hit me exactly where I would hurt most. Those children are my one true joy in life. They grow up so fast, and every single moment I get to spend with them is precious.

I'm stuck between the proverbial rock and hard place. Hobson's choice, if you will. "Let me make this perfectly clear," I say, rising from my chair. "It is under protest that I will acquiesce to your demand." And with that I turn on my heel and storm from the room. They got what they wanted, and I need to be alone so I can think.

Damn them to hell for qualifying their demand. While there are any number of women I've socialised with in one manner or another, the pool shrinks significantly once the term *suitable* is applied.

"You okay?" Craig asks on our way to the car.

"Not even close to it."

"If you need to talk…"

"Thanks." He's been more than a bodyguard to me over the years. He's proven he can keep a confidence, and he has been steadfast in his loyalty. I know he'd take a bullet for me because that's what he gets paid for. But he's also gone well above and beyond his job description. Covered for me when he could have, rightly, told me to go fuck myself. Provided an ear and advice whenever I've needed it.

I'm not ready to talk yet. I need to wrap my head around it all first. And even then, I might not be up for a discussion.

"Are you in for the night?" Craig asks as he locks the door behind us.

"Yeah, I am."

"Then I'll see you in the morning. But if you need to talk, you know where to find me."

"Thanks, Craig. I'm fine. Enjoy what's left of your evening."

Grabbing a bottle of Black Sheep and a packet of cheese and onion crisps, I retire to my own room.

After I've had a few sips of my beer and a handful of crisps, I pull out my phone and fire up Fetwrk.

If I'm going to be stuck with a wife, she may as well be one I'm willing to fuck for the rest of my life. Because for all my bad boy ways, I'm faithful. I won't fuck around, and I won't accept any less from my wife.

SEVEN

Charlotte

One of my meetings is cancelled at the last minute, leaving me time to have a quick pub lunch with Tilda.

"So, what came up last night that was more important than an evening on the town with me?" I tease as soon as she joins me at the small table by the window.

"If only it were as exciting as your out-of-control imagination would have you believe. Ten minutes before it was time to go home, my bloody boss decided he needed my project finished for first thing this morning. A project that he'd told me wouldn't be due until next bloody week."

"Oh, Tilda, that's terrible. If memory serves, he's done this to you before, yes?"

"A few times. If I could get away with it, I would absolutely tell him to take his job and shove it right up his hairy bum. Unfortunately, I'm not in a position to be unemployed, nor are there any new job prospects on the horizon—the downside to refining my area of expertise to such a niche sector. So, I shall tough it out."

My heart breaks for her. We met at Lady Bart's. She was there on a scholarship—I swear, she's the brainiest person I know—and I was there because that's where all the Grey girls are educated. Neither of us really fit in with the rest of the girls, so we were a clique of two. And that suited us just fine. My social status protected me from most unkindness, which in turn helped protect Tilda.

She and I went to different universities—she to Oxford and I to the University of Edinburgh—but we've remained in close contact and see each other as often as possible.

"So, what did you get up to last night while I was toiling away on that project?"

Heat rises up my neck to my hairline, and from the burn in my ears, I know they must be scarlet.

"Oh, clearly you had an excellent night. Considering you didn't set up a safe-call, can I assume it was—"

"Yes," I interrupt. "It was, now shush."

"Ah," she says, and taps her nose. "I'm glad your evening in town wasn't a complete waste, then."

"I'm glad my meeting got cancelled so you and I could have a catch-up."

"Me, too. Are you still checking out that pony this afternoon?" she asks.

"Yes. I hope this is the one. They've been looking for so long, and it breaks my heart to keep telling wee Pippa that this isn't the right pony for her. This one will be the sixth I've been asked to assess for her, and she's been so patient, but I can hardly bear to see the disappointment in her eyes every time I give her the bad news."

"And a pony is really going to help?"

"I don't know. But after the year she's had..."

"Hopefully, this one works out."

"Yeah. Meanwhile, any interesting hook-ups lately?"

When Mel Seymour set me up with Fetwrk, I made sure to arrange for Tilda to get it, too. Even though she's not a public figure of any sort, she's my best friend, she's probably kinkier than me, and it was important to me that she be protected.

"One or two, but I've been so bogged down with work, I don't get much chance to go out—as evidenced by last night's surprise deadline."

I wish there was something I could do to help get Tilda out of her insane employment situation, but the reality is, I don't have the right kind of connections.

Nearly forty-five minutes later, Tilda looks at her watch and starts gathering her things. "Sorry, babes, I must dash. I don't dare be late back."

"Go. We'll get together again soon."

With a hug and a kiss on my cheek, she races back to work.

Taking the final swig of my ginger ale, I head off too.

It's an uneventful drive to the stable. Once I'm out of the city and off the motorway, there is very little traffic. And even though it's a grey day, it's not rainy, which will make my job more pleasant.

Alfie and Pippa are waiting in the stable yard when I arrive. "I'm sorry, am I late?"

"Oh, heavens no. We're early." I don't need to ask why. Sweet little Pippa is practically bouncing with excitement.

God, I hope I don't have to disappoint her again.

"Charlotte, this is Margaret Smythe."

I offer my hand "Lovely to meet you,"

"You too," she says as we shake. "I'm sure you're busy, so shall we get on?"

The moment I run my hands down the pony's back legs, I know I'm about to disappoint Pippa again. And it breaks my heart. But we shouldn't have even got this far in the process.

"I'm sorry. I'm sure he's a very sweet boy, but he's not sound. In fact, I recommend you have your own vet examine him."

"You don't know what you're talking about. He's perfectly sound."

I don't listen to her. I just grab Alfie's sleeve and walk back to where we're parked. "I'll meet you at the house, and we'll talk," I tell him as I get in my car, grateful that Margaret Smythe didn't follow us the entire way.

Fortunately, my cousin's farm is on the way home. Twenty-five minutes later, I pull into the yard behind his Land Rover.

"Stay to tea?" he asks.

"I should be getting home, but yes, I'd like that."

Once we're in the kitchen, Alfie puts the kettle on

and starts preparing the meal. "Would you like some help?" I offer.

"No, better you have that chat with Pippa, yeah?"

Nodding, I invite Pippa to sit on my lap. "I'm sorry I had to say no to that pony, too. You've been so patient, and I really, really wanted him to be just right for you."

"I know. It's like I'm Goldilocks looking for just right."

"It is. And you are the most wonderful Goldilocks in the history of all Goldilocks," I tell her with a big squeeze.

"I just feel bad that he has to stay there with that mean lady."

"Me, too." And in that moment, I know I'm going to be spending money I can ill-afford for an unsound pony to be living out the rest of his days at my sanctuary. "Do you think maybe he should come live with me and keep Maisie company?"

Alfie gives me a you're-such-a-pushover look as he shakes his head.

"Yay! I think that's perfect."

I leave shortly after we eat. It's already dark, and I'm going to be arriving home much later than planned. Even though I'd texted Darren and he told me to take my time, I still feel guilty. Guilty for rushing out on Alfie and Pippa, guilty for Darren being the responsible human for longer than he's supposed to be.

Just guilty.

Kevin races to greet me as soon as I'm out of my car, his ridiculous little stump of a tail wagging at a blurring speed.

"Hello, my boy. I missed you. Were you good for Darren?"

"He was. He's always a good boy."

"Thank you again, Darren. You will take tomorrow off, won't you?"

"I will. Have a good evening."

"You, too."

Kevin and I go indoors where I unpack and start a load of laundry. Oh, if the girls from school could see just how glamorous my life is. I laugh.

Most of the girls in our class did as expected and married well, produced the requisite number of offspring having never cooked a meal, cleaned a toilet, or operated a washing machine in their lives.

And that's just fine with me. I wouldn't change a thing.

Sure, I'm lonely sometimes, and think it would be nice to have someone to spend my evenings with and sex on the regular.

But with companions come compromise. And am I really prepared to adjust the way I live to accommodate a man?

Maybe one day, if I don't get too cemented in my ways, but for now, I have a drawer full of sex toys for the day to day, and when I need an honest to goodness kinky human interaction...I have an app for that.

EIGHT

Duncan

The next morning, I wade through Fetwrk reassessing all the women I've hooked up with over the past year. And the only option reasonably available to me is exactly the same as it was last night.

Lady Charlotte Grey.

"Craig," I call out from the living room.

"Yes?"

"I still don't want to talk about it, but needs must and all that. I've been ordered to find a suitable wife and marry her within the year."

"I see." Craig does an admirable job at not reacting, for which I'm grateful. "And?"

"Options are slim."

"But you've narrowed it down."

I nod. "Lady Charlotte Grey. I know you've already done a background check on her, but given the circumstances, I require a more extensive one. I need to know everything there is about her. Every skeleton in her closet. Every possible risk of exploitation. As soon as humanly possible."

"I'll get right on it." He gives me a pointed look.

"Would it make it easier to speed that job along if I were to stay home today?"

"So much easier."

I take myself off to my study and settle in to get some work done and try to take my mind off this untenable position I've been forced into.

A little over four hours later, Craig knocks on the doorframe and peeks his head in.

"Is now a good time?"

"Absolutely. Come in."

As soon as he's settled in the seat across from me, he opens a folder.

"My god, there's not much to tell. She's kept her nose exceptionally clean. There was one incident requiring Winston Frobisher."

"Interesting. Do you have any details on that?"

"No. However she activated a profile on Fetwrk right around the same time, so I don't think it's too difficult to piece the story together."

"No, I suppose not. Do you think it's important for us to find out exactly what happened?"

"If Frobisher took care of it, then it should be well handled. And it's probably better if you get the story directly from Lady Charlotte on her own terms."

"Yes, that might be for the best. What else is there?"

She has a friend, Tilda Roberts, who she went to school with. She's managed to keep herself out of trouble, too. But as a scholarship student at Lady Bartholemew's, I suspect perhaps it's more out of habit. Careful to not risk losing her scholarship, and once that was no longer a concern, she just continued on that straight and narrow rather than rebel. That said, she's also on Fetwrk, so I suspect there's some bad girl in there somewhere, she's just making sure to accommodate that part of herself in a way that's less likely to cause her grief down the road."

"You seem to know an awful lot about this Tilda person." Craig's face pinkens slightly, and I let it go at that. "Back to Lady Charlotte, then."

"She's estranged from her brother—her only immediate family—and she is in dire financial straits."

I consider the last part. Money trouble is always excellent leverage. And I have a feeling I'm going to need leverage to get what I need from Charlotte.

"She's a fully qualified veterinarian, but she doesn't have a practice, as such." I lift an eyebrow. "She mostly limits her skills to her animal rescue sanctuary, and a few others."

"The sanctuary would be the reason for her financial difficulties, I assume."

"Yes. It runs at a significant deficit. Apparently, Lady Charlotte has been known to sell items of value whenever the sanctuary is on the verge of being evicted."

I make a mental note to arrange to buy back as many of Charlotte's belongings as possible. I don't doubt that a great many of them will have more than monetary value to her.

"Is there anything else of importance I should know?"

"I think those are the highlights."

"Thank you for taking care of this so quickly. I appreciate it."

"Well, you are under a bit of a time constraint. Is there anything else you need from me?"

"Maybe just find me the name of someone I can hire to find and recover the items Lady Charlotte was compelled to sell."

"Happy to. She's really a lovely person. I think you've chosen well."

"Thanks, Craig. You've been a great friend to me all these years, and I truly value your opinion."

"Are you still staying in?"

"Yes. I have a lot of planning to do before I propose to the lovely Lady Charlotte Grey."

NINE

Charlotte

I'm entirely speechless.

I've had him repeat himself three times already because I was certain he must be playing a practical joke. A joke that is in particularly poor taste. Even for him.

"It's the perfect set up."

I raise an eyebrow and wait a beat. "How so?"

"Well, first of all, your family must be all over you to marry by now. And of course, the expectation is for you to marry as far above your station as possible—improve the family pedigree and all that." I keep my expression blank, even though I'm seething. He's not wrong on either count and that annoys me no end. "And let's face it, you can't marry any higher up than me. All the good princes are taken, and my eldest brother has already produced his heir and spare."

"Even if my family were pushing for me to marry,

and above my station at that, I have no interest in marrying you, and there is nothing you can say or do that would change my mind."

I dislike the nasty gleam in his eye, and I silently run back through our conversation so far, searching for something I could have possibly said that could give him an upper hand—

"Your animal rescue sanctuary seems to be in serious financial trouble..."

He leaves that just hanging there, and my heart sinks deep into my belly. He's zeroed in on the one thing in this life I truly care about.

"What are you offering?" I ask.

"A trust that will provide full funding for your organisation in perpetuity, providing I hold position on the board of directors—you would benefit greatly from my expertise—we can revisit this stipulation after one year."

Ugh. That ego of his is unbelievable. However, he's proven himself to be highly successful in the business world, so he could actually be an asset on a couple of fronts...

"And?"

"Freedom to do exactly as you like outside of familial obligations and marital fidelity."

"And?"

"And what? Most women of your social standing would be thrilled at the prospect of marrying a prince, full stop."

"I'm not most women."

"Clearly."

"And in exchange for your *generosity...*?" I brace for what I am sure will be an extortionate cost.

"In public, you and I portray the very definition of a blissfully happy and respectable married couple. In private, we do whatever we want with the exception of sex. That remains in-house. No matter what, we both are to be completely faithful to one another. And while we're on the subject of sex, I'm going to need a lot of it—the kinkier the better. You have until morning to accept. If you don't, we renegotiate. However, if it comes to that, I can assure you, the new terms will be less enticing."

"If I *did* agree to your terms, how would it all play out?"

"We will gradually start appearing together at social functions, but nothing I wouldn't normally attend. We don't want to raise eyebrows any more than necessary. When asked, we can say, without stretching the truth too far, that we'd been seeing each other casually for quite some time. We get engaged in a little under six months, married a few months after that, and then continue on with our lives."

"And other than sex and public couple time, I'm free to do as I please?"

"Kinky sex whenever and however I want it, and respectable, happily married public couple time. Beyond that, yes, it's up to you how you conduct your life as long as it's completely scandal-free. If you create a scandal, or even the potential for a scandal, you will be severely punished. You have until tomorrow morning to give me your answer."

I want to tell him to take his bullshit deal and shove it up his ass and forget he ever met me. But I can't because I have an animal rescue that desperately needs funding and quite frankly, the prospect of a life of satisfying kinky sex and some civilised social engagements is far more appealing than the inevitability of my money issues forcing me back under my brother's control. Walking away from *him* meant giving up access to my trust fund. As for scandals? That's always been more Duncan's thing than mine.

The hefty rent due on the first of every month for the property that provides sanctuary to the multitude of rescued animals is crippling on its own. Add occasional specialised veterinary care I am unable to provide on top of the cost of feed, equipment, and supplies, and there's only one answer I can give Duncan.

"Yes. I'll do it."

And I will probably spend the rest of my life regretting those words.

TEN

Duncan

Five months later

I CAN HARDLY BELIEVE how smoothly it has all gone. I am still a royal pariah, as far as public opinion is concerned, but the process of improving my status has been going well, albeit more slowly than ideal.

It wasn't until the fourth event Charlotte accompanied me to that the press paid any real attention to my date. Fortunately, this gave Charlotte a small taste of what life in the public eye is like before becoming tabloid fodder.

Since then, she's been on the front page of every news outlet in the country, almost daily.

I'm impressed with how well she's stood up to it. In fact, she's done an excellent job of twisting their attention to her animal rescue organisation, which inevitably sends the reporters off in search of something more titillating to present to the salivating public.

By the end of our first month of officially dating, I'd arranged the funding for her sanctuary, made the appropriate alterations at Finleigh Park, and moved her menagerie to their new home.

Relocating the sanctuary to my estate just north of London was a surprise for her, and I have to admit, her delight and gratitude made me feel better than I had in a long, long time.

When I first bought the estate, I expected I'd live in the manor house with all the staff and trappings.

However, Charlotte pointed out that it would be next to impossible to keep an active, kinky sex life on the down-low in a heavily staffed residence. No matter how carefully you have them vetted, there is always someone willing to sell another's private life to the tabloids.

"We can live quite comfortably in the dower house," she'd said. "We can see to our own day-to-day needs and have staff from the manor come in once a week to do a proper clean. I'm sure they won't consider it odd to have some rooms, like our offices and bedrooms, locked and off-limits."

In the end, I wisely set my ego aside and conceded that she was right. Now I'm living in the dower house and rent out the manor, fully staffed, as a sort of high-end AirBnB.

Today, however, is the real test.

I'm taking her to *officially* meet my parents.

This is make or break. If they don't approve, I'm fucked, because I do not have a backup plan. Which is likely why I've left it so long. Put them in the position where they're likely to feel obligated to approve. And really, given the timeline they've given me, bringing my future bride for approval much before now would have set alarm bells ringing. Best to think positively and trust that it will all be fine.

Charlotte walks out her door the moment Craig and I arrive to pick her up. The fact that she's obviously been watching for us pleases me more than it probably should.

"Ready?" I ask as she settles into the back seat of the car with me.

"As I'll ever be, I suppose."

"It'll be fine. Just be yourself and they'll love you." I try to feel as confident as I sound.

We spend the rest of the drive wrapped up in our own thoughts. I'd already schooled her as best I could on what to expect. Of course, having never brought a woman home for approval before, I could only base my knowledge on what transpired when my brothers brought someone home for the parental blessing.

I'm only slightly grateful for the informality of the family salon because, again, it's brimming with siblings.

"Mother, Father, may I present Lady Charlotte Grey."

Charlotte curtsies prettily for my parents and my chest swells with pride.

My father crooks his finger. "Come closer. Grey, is it?"

"Yes, Your Majesty."

"Your brother is Richard, Earl of Warrington?"

"He is," she says, flushing a dark red from the neck up.

"I see."

Oh. Shit. The disapproval in his tone is unmistakable.

Charlotte's expression remains neutral, but her shoulders slump a little, and I'm at a loss for how to help.

"Never mind," my father says cheerfully. "We can't choose our blood, can we?" He winks at her, nods his head towards me, and she visibly relaxes.

With that awkwardness over, my family is quick to accept Charlotte into the fold. Just before she and I are about to take our leave, my mother pulls me aside. "Charlotte seems like an excellent match for you, Duncan. Do not mess this up."

"I'll do my best."

"See that you do. There is a lot riding on the outcome."

ELEVEN

Charlotte

Shortly after all the introductions are over, the door opens and the salon is invaded by a small herd of children, who immediately mob Duncan. I try to shift away to a quiet corner of the room, but no such luck.

"Right you lot, come and meet Charlotte."

"Is she your girlfriend?" Frederick, the oldest asks in a loud stage-whisper. One advantage to these children being famous is I already know who is who. There's nothing worse than meeting a large group of people at once and trying to remember everyone's name.

"She certainly is, Freddie," Duncan stage-whispers back.

"Are you going to be my auntie?" Daniel asks. "I already have four aunties and I'm four years old." I wasn't actually expecting to meet the younger members of the family today, and I am not prepared for precocious questions.

"Well—"

"If she were, how many aunties would you have?" Duncan holds up four fingers. "Four aunties now, plus one new auntie..." he holds up a finger on his other hand.

Daniel carefully counts each finger. "Five," he shouts. I will have five whole aunties."

"I'm going to get a new auntie." He's not wrong, but it feels too soon.

"Truly, Duncle?" Freddie asks.

Smiling, Duncan gives my hand a squeeze. "Truly."

Joey, who is also four, tugs on my sleeve and looks up at me with the most adorably serious expression. "I think you should give Nanna a girl baby. She only has boy babies, and I think she would like a girl baby. Except I prefer boy babies. But it would be okay for you to give her one girl baby."

Duncan laughs and sweeps the wee boy up into his arms. "You, my young sir, are awfully cheeky."

"Duncle?"

"Yes, Bertie?"

"When is the next boys' night? It's been an awfully long time since our last one."

"You're right, it has been a long time." Duncan pulls his phone from his pocket. "I'm setting a reminder right now to make arrangements with your parents."

"But they're right here. You could—"

"I understand, but I find it is usually better to not put parents on the spot about these kinds of things."

Bertie lets out a deep huff. "Okay. But you promise you'll talk to them?"

"As soon as I can, and we'll pick the very first date we're all available. Okay?"

"Okay."

I look at Duncan and lift an eyebrow in question.

"Every so often, the six boys come to mine for a sleepover. We watch films, play games, and eat far too much junk food."

"Last time, Thomas got sick," Daniel chimes in, a look of pure glee on his face. "That was when Duncle rented the bouncy castle—"

"Wait," Freddie interrupts, "if you get married, what happens to boys' night?"

"I should hope it continues," I answer. "I'm certain I could make sure to be elsewhere on those occasions."

Duncan gives me an approving nod. "Charlotte is right, boys' night will continue as normal."

"What if you have a girl baby?" Joey asks. He certainly seems obsessed over there being a girl baby.

I allow myself the small indulgence of a fantasy. "Then she and I shall have girls' nights."

"Oh, Auntie Xandra could come. I think she might like girls' night." James says.

"Don't get ahead of yourselves, you lot. Before there is even the possibility for any of those things to happen, Charlotte has to marry me."

"Hurry up. I need new cousins," Joey says. "I'm tired of being the youngest."

Ah, that explains a lot.

At that point, Duncan makes our excuses and we leave.

"I'm sorry. I didn't think the children would be quite that..."

"It's fine. They're children. They speak their minds and they were delightful."

"And you won't mind boys' nights?"

"Don't be ridiculous. Of course, I won't mind. They clearly love spending time with you, and I hope maybe once we're married, they will be keen to spend time with both of us."

TWELVE

Charlotte

I'd imagined my wedding day countless times as a young girl, complete with Prince Charming.

Today resembles none of that.

True, there is a prince. But charming?

Not even close.

As the fifth son of the reigning monarch, and still the most publicly reviled member of the royal family, we opted for a very quiet, close family- and friends-only affair in the little village church near Finleigh Park.

Craig fought fiercely against our choice of venue. He called it a security nightmare, a terror attack just waiting to happen. But in the end, he gave in to our wishes and made it work.

Instead of my beloved father escorting me to the church in the horse and carriage I'd always dreamed of, I'm riding solo in the back of a very nice Rolls Royce.

My brother, Richard, Earl of Warrington—who I privately refer to as The Dick of Warrington—had some lofty expectation that he'd accompany me and give me away. Not even if my life depended on it. I know he just wanted to exploit the connection and I was having none of it. He didn't even receive an invitation, and I was more than happy to take the resulting backlash at the slight.

My dress, however is perfectly lovely.

Quite possibly the only part of today that is exactly how I want it. Sometimes we must treasure every bright spot that comes our way, no matter how small.

I wanted it to be just Duncan and me standing at the front of the church with the vicar.

But Duncan wanted all his nieces and nephews in the wedding party, and I couldn't deny all those sweet children an opportunity to dress up and be part of their favourite uncle's *special* day.

And if we were having a wedding party for this sham of a marriage anyway, it only made sense that I would have Tilda, my closest friend as my maid of honour and Pippa as a bridesmaid.

However, if I must walk down the aisle, I will do it entirely on my own. Because that is how I am entering into this marriage.

Alone, with no family.

Duncan chose his twin sister as his best person. As he put it, she was the only sibling who had yet to betray him.

As I pull up in front of the church, I clear my head of everything except the day ahead and how I shall do everything in my power to enjoy it despite the cage it represents.

Ailsa, my bodyguard, holds the door open, and Tilda helps me out of the car before straightening my dress.

"It's not too late to back out," she whispers. And that right there is one of the many reasons I love her. She knows nothing about the agreement Duncan and I have. Other than being one of the very few who knows that *seeing each other casually* really meant Duncan and I hooked up a number of times through Fetwrk, she's been given the same cock and bull story the rest of the world has. Fairytale romance, blah, blah, blah.

"I'm fine. But thanks for having my back," I tell her as I pull her in for a hug.

"Then let's go get you married."

We climb the church steps together and we're greeted at the entrance by the royal brood and my own dear Pippa, all dressed in their finery, excitement shooting off them like sparks from a bonfire.

Tilda wrangles them into position, and once the music changes, she sends them off in turn down the aisle.

"Last chance," she tells me just before it's her turn to go.

Smiling, I shake my head and shoo her along with a hand gesture.

After taking one last, deep breath of freedom, I take my first step towards the rest of my life.

THIRTEEN

Duncan

"You may kiss your bride."

Finally, the words I've been waiting to hear all fucking day.

I pull Charlotte in for a long, deep kiss. A small taste of what's to come.

Married.

The entire business was surreal. I found it oddly endearing when she stumbled a little over the *love, cherish, and obey* part. She'd agreed to the inclusion of *obey* in her vows. Actually, I made it clear to her that it was non-negotiable.

I'll admit to being uncomfortable at promising a love I don't feel.

That doesn't stop me from calculating exactly how long I must wait until I can respectably whisk her from the reception and take her—mind, body, and soul.

My original wedding night plan was to drag Charlotte directly to the dungeon, but when my sister asked me what romantic gestures I have planned for when I bring Charlotte home tonight—there went dark and dirty.

True, Charlotte would have been completely onboard with me taking her to the dungeon, but regardless of how big an asshole I am, it's her wedding night, and the only one she's ever going to have, so I altered my plans accordingly.

"You're mine, now. Whenever, wherever, and however I want." I whisper in her ear as we turn to make our way back through the church.

Her breath catches and her gaze flicks up to mine and I quirk an expectant eyebrow.

"Yes, Sir," she whispers back. Her voice is sultry, and my dick is instantly hard.

I tuck her arm in my elbow and escort her back down the aisle, accepting well-wishes from our guests along the way.

Outside the church we're required to pose for photographs. So many bloody photographs.

FOURTEEN

Charlotte

Once the photographer releases us from the interminable photo shoot, Duncan and I are driven the short distance to the reception at Finleigh Park in the Rolls I arrived at the church in.

"I kept my promise these past two months. And as soon as we're free to leave this bloody soiree, you are mine whenever, however, and wherever the mood strikes me for the rest of our lives."

His breath on my ear sends delicious shivers down my spine. I really shouldn't be turned on by what he's saying, but it's been ages since we've had sex of any sort, and no matter what the rest of married life will be, I'm confident sex between us will remain off the charts.

"Let us go and make merry with our guests."

Of course, there were more photos. Everything must be thoroughly documented for some sort of posterity, I suppose. And organising group shots takes so much longer when there is a herd of small children to wrangle into place and get smiling at the same time.

By the time it's all done, I am absolutely ravenous. I hadn't eaten a thing all day. My belly was too full of butterflies to leave room for sustenance.

Duncan offers his arm and we lead our guests into the dining room. When we were planning our wedding, Duncan and I wanted a morning ceremony followed by a luncheon so we could be done with all this nonsense by mid-afternoon, but his mother overruled us, insisting that it was thoroughly unreasonable to expect a bride to be up at the crack of dawn and rushing around on her wedding day.

Given I needed to be up by eight this morning in order to be on time, I'm grateful for her foresight and wisdom.

Fortunately, because we are only entertaining those closest to us, supper is a very informal affair. Yes, the table is dressed to the nines, but we opted for a self-serve buffet rather than a multi-course silver-service affair.

The best part of the entire meal is the children. They make what could have been a tedious, boring chore into a delightful evening of love and laughter.

While we're eating, Joey comes around and climbs into Duncan's lap. "Auntie Charlotte married you. Can I have that new cousin now?"

Surprisingly, Duncan doesn't chuckle along with those sitting near us. "Having babies is serious business that takes a lot of thought and consideration. Charlotte and I still need some time figuring out how to live with each other before we consider bringing a whole new person into the family. You wouldn't want a baby to come before we're all ready, would you?"

"I guess not." His poor little face falls. "Maybe one of the other aunties and uncles will make me a new cousin." And with that, he jumps off Duncan's lap and sets off on a mission.

My heart cracks in two. I don't delude myself into thinking I will ever be a mother.

Duncan and I do not, nor will we ever, have the kind of relationship that would be healthy to bring children into. The thought makes me a little sad, but I have my animals, and while they will never be a substitute, they do give me some sense of fulfilment.

What makes me sadder still about the prospect of never having children is that Duncan won't be a father.

He is a completely different person when he is with children. He's loving and doting and patient, and oh, so kind.

It's a side of him I only ever see when he is with his nieces and nephews, and I wish I got to see more of it. I suppose I will, if we can arrange for the children to come spend time with us once we're settled.

When we're finished eating, Duncan leans in close to me. "Are you ready to cut the cake?"

"Yes."

Taking my hand, he leads me to the small table at the far end of the room where our wedding cake awaits.

He picks up the knife and wraps my hand around the

handle before covering it with his. Then, after we've cut the first two pieces, I panic. What if he does that awful smash cake in my face thing?

"Charlotte," he whispers, holding a small piece of cake near my lips. "Trust me."

I open my mouth and take the cake from his fingers.

"My turn," I say after finishing my mouthful.

He gently sucks my fingertips as he takes the cake from them and all I want right this minute is for him to drag me off to the nearest empty room and fuck me stupid.

"Soon, sweetheart. We're nearly done with our obligations."

FIFTEEN

Charlotte

Duncan wanted to go away on a honeymoon. He was convinced it was necessary to start our marriage off right.

I wanted to take that time to settle in at Finleigh Park.

On this, I fought him until I won.

So, when we leave the reception in the big house, instead of driving to the airport, we take a long, quiet stroll down to the dower house.

"How are you doing, Charlotte?"

His question surprises me. I didn't expect him to show any tender feelings. I want to be snarky, but it is my wedding day, such as it is, and I'm sure there will be no shortage of things I will have good reason to be snarky with him over in the years ahead.

"I'm tired."

"Not too tired, I hope."

"No, not too tired."

"I'll make it a short but hard session, tonight. We can take our time tomorrow, after we've both had a good rest."

"That would be lovely, thank you."

"I'm dying to rip that dress off you, but I suppose you have some sentimental attachment."

"I would prefer you didn't rip it. My underthings are fair game, though, if that helps."

His grin is feral. "I think that will suffice."

As soon as we reach the dower house, he scoops me into his arms. "I know you didn't want this. Neither of us did. But I will do the best I can for both of us, and I hope you will too."

"I'll do my best."

"Welcome home, dearest," he says as he carries me through the front door. I fully expect him to put me down the moment he's kicked it shut and we are no longer at risk of being seen or photographed. Instead he continues walking towards the stairs.

"What are you doing? Put me down."

"No."

"Duncan, Sir, please? You're going to hurt yourself," I tell him as he ascends the stairs.

"Are you saying I'm weak?"

"No, Sir. Of course not."

"Then what could have you so concerned for my welfare?"

"I'm not exactly—"

"I'm going to stop you right there before you say something we'll both regret. This is your wedding day.

The only one you are going to get, and I intend to do it as right as I am able."

"Thank you, Sir."

When he bursts through our bedroom door, I'm overcome with emotion. There are lit candles dotted around and a bottle of champagne is chilling on the bedside table.

I don't ask the question that's burning my tongue because I don't know that I really want to know the answer.

"It's lovely."

"It's not the honeymoon suite in a swank hotel that I wanted for us," he whispers as he lays me gently on the bed.

"It's better."

"I was terrified you were going to need to come in here today and spoil my surprise. I wanted to light the candles myself, too, but there was no way I could sneak off for that, so I had to rely on my sister."

"It's a truly wonderful surprise. Thank you."

"I wasn't joking about a short, hard session tonight. I was only going to give you five with the cane, before I ravage you, but you are so beautiful, I've been fighting a raging hard-on since the second you started walking down the aisle. So, for making me suffer most uncomfortably for hours, you will have another five cane strokes before I make you mine forever. Now, let's get you out of this lovely dress while I still have the patience."

I try not to giggle.

He motions for me to get up and I stand and turn very slowly in front of him.

"Fuck. Me. How many buttons are there?"

"You'd have to ask Tilda. She did them up."

"That's five more strokes for the extra time this is going to take."

"Yes, Sir. Thank you, Sir."

He starts at the top, grumbling as he undoes each button, and I find it ridiculously endearing.

"Surely, this must be far enough," he says when he's about halfway down. I slip the top of the dress off my shoulders and down my arms.

"Damn, not quite. Hold on a moment. We don't want to pop any of these."

Four buttons later, my dress slides down over my hips and puddles on the floor. I step out of it, and before I can bend down, Duncan has already snatched it up and is walking toward the wardrobe. "Bend over the end of the bed while I hang this up. And leave the shoes on."

The bed is higher off the ground than most, so even with my heels on, it's nearly waist high. I don't doubt it's been purpose built.

"So beautiful." He steps in close behind me, reaching around and cupping my breasts. "How many strokes, Charlotte?"

"Fifteen, Sir."

"You'll be a good girl and thank me for each one."

His warmth disappears as he yanks my knickers down to my mid-thigh.

"Oh, that is such a sexy sight."

The first strike of the cane comes before I expect it, landing across the fullest part of my ass, and it takes me a bit to catch my breath. "Thank you, Sir."

"I've changed my mind. You can thank me at the end. I don't have the patience to draw this out, so I'm going to make this fast. However, tomorrow morning, you can expect another fifteen, with which I will take my sweet time. Understood?"

"Yes, Sir. Thank you, Sir."

The cane whizzes through the air a split second before landing each stripe across my ass and they come so fast, I barely register the pain before the next falls.

"What do you say?" he asks. I'm all floaty and it seems almost like he'd only just started.

"You're done already?"

He chuckles. "I could go on, if you'd prefer..."

"Thank you, Sir. Thank you."

"Good girl. Now, don't move."

I consider his demand a kindness. My ass is a burning mess right now, so bent over the end of the bed is probably the most comfortable position I could ask for.

SIXTEEN

Charlotte

Duncan greets me with the feral grin as I enter the sitting room. "Over," he demands, pointing to the back of the overstuffed leather settee.

"Duncan, we'll be late." We're supposed to be attending a reception for some foreign dignitary at the palace. We've been married barely two months and we've already been required to attend more functions than we had during the entire nine months prior to our wedding.

"And the longer it takes for you to obey..."

He lets the rest of that sentence hang in the air between us. We've been down this road before.

Letting out a heavy sigh, I carefully position myself to avoid crumpling the fabric of my dress as much as possible. Some wrinkles are entirely too obvious. I make a mental note to stick to fabrics and designs that are more forgiving of my husband's propensity for a last-minute fuck prior to public appearances.

Cool air hits the bare tops of my thighs as he shimmies the skirt of my dress up and over my back. He touches the tip of his cock to my entrance, grasps the top of my shoulders and slams into me. Each thrust pushes the sofa forward, and I have no doubt there will be bruises where my body meets the sofa back.

It's not the rough sex I resent.

Never that.

It's the humiliation of arriving late with my dress in a state where I'm convinced everyone in the room can tell exactly why we were delayed. Sure, we're married, and everyone knows married people have sex. But that doesn't stop me feeling self-conscious and embarrassed about it being obvious.

"Come on, he says," as he pulls out and slaps my ass. "We don't want to arrive too much later."

Once we're in the car and on our way, he opens his trousers. "Fuck me hard with your mouth. And I recommend you show your enthusiasm. It would be a shame for you to arrive with your hair in disarray because you required assistance."

Not to mention even more humiliating. I rearrange myself and don't hesitate take him fully into my mouth and down my throat.

Normally, I like to tease him a little. Enough for him to get all caveman about it. But there's only so much humiliation I can stand, and arriving at the palace with blow-job hair is well beyond my limit, so I bob my way up and down his shaft as hard and fast as I can. I'm quietly triumphant when only a few minutes later, he grabs the back of my neck and thrusts deep as he comes down my throat.

"Good girl."

And with that, we're done talking to each other.

SEVENTEEN

Duncan

After just over two months of marriage and a number of hiccoughs along the way, Charlotte and I have finally settled into an uneasy kind of normal.

Basically, we stay out of each other's way and lead our own lives, except for social obligations and sex. She presents to me whenever and wherever I order her to. And while she does have her own bedroom, I don't allow her to sleep in it.

She's accepted that my word is law and I will brook no argument. In return, I don't interfere with the day-to-day running of the sanctuary.

That is, until today.

I handle the business end of things and let her know how much discretionary funding she has available each month after expenses are paid. The understanding was that she would run the sanctuary within its means.

Grabbing my mobile off my desk, I call Charlotte.

"Duncan," she says, sounding a little out of breath. "I'll ring you back, I'm rather tied up at the moment."

I'll give her bloody tied up.

"No, you will not ring me back. You will do whatever is necessary to be in my office and kneeling at my feet within the next fifteen minutes." I may be a demanding bastard, but I am willing to give her a *little* flexibility when I know she's working with the animals.

While I wait, I poke through the toy cupboard in my office and pull out a few things.

Fourteen minutes after I called, Charlotte comes racing into my office. "I was right in the middle of—"

"Whenever, and wherever, Charlotte. That was the agreement. And you do not appear to be on your knees..." I look pointedly down at the floor in front of me.

She hurries over and kneels quite gracefully.

"I was just going through the sanctuary finances for last month..." I trail off, watching her carefully to assess whether her overspending was an oversight or deliberate.

Her expression would have given her away if her guilty blush hadn't already done so.

"I was clear about how much money was available to you, yet you appear to have spent nearly twice that."

"I'm sorry, I—"

"I did set up a healthy contingency fund. Why didn't you come to me?"

"You might have said no."

"Yes, I might have. You'll never know, now. And on

top of that, you've got a punishment coming because you clearly knew you required permission."

"Duncan—"

"No, Charlotte. No excuses. No justifications. You have a generous budget, and the time to make your case was *before* you overspent. You thought it would be better to ask forgiveness than permission? We shall see if you still feel that way after your punishment is over. Stand up and strip."

She rises and quickly removes her clothing. Wisely, she seems to be taking her situation seriously. I snatch up her knickers and place them in my pocket.

"Turn around and grab your ankles."

She presents her ass to me, and her naughty little pussy is glistening. I press the Bluetooth ben wa balls deep inside her, and then clamp her labia with this nifty stainless-steel device I found while trolling the internet a few weeks ago.

It consists of inner and outer ellipses. The outer part goes around the outside of her pussy, and the inner part nests between her outer and inner pussy lips. I tighten the screws at the top and bottom of the contraption until her outer lips are snugly trapped.

"You will finish your chores like this, wearing only your work trousers. You'll soon discover you won't be able to just close your legs to hold the ben wa balls in. And with no knickers to help you, you'll be completely reliant on your inner muscles to keep the balls from falling down your trouser leg. And Charlotte, let me be clear, the balls had best not fall."

"Yes, Sir."

"One more thing. You are not to come."

Picking up her trousers, I root through the pockets for her mobile. I download the app and sync it to both the ben wa balls and my own mobile.

"You will keep this with you at all times," I tell her as I slip it back into her pocket

"Yes, Sir."

"Now get dressed and off you go."

"Thank you, Sir."

"Don't thank me yet. This is just the first part of your punishment. I'm well aware you have things that must be taken care of, but I want you to spend the time you are doing them fully aware that the rest of your day and evening are fully booked."

"Yes, Sir."

"Report to me as soon as you've completed what must be done."

"Yes, Sir."

"And Charlotte—do not dally."

EIGHTEEN

Charlotte

The contraption Duncan has set up is deliciously devious. Discreet enough that nobody can tell it's there, yet it feels like there's an entire scaffolding between my legs. It's also a little heavy, so it's not only pinching my labia, gravity is stretching them.

My clit is aching for some friction, and this thing makes it impossible for me to even surreptitiously rub my thighs together.

I'm barely out the front door when the balls start buzzing wildly, and all I can do is stand still, clenching my pussy in desperation and hoping they don't vibrate their way out.

Mercifully, it doesn't last long, but I realise I'm going to have to find a way to deal with this until I've finished in the barns where there are other people working.

Why didn't I just go ask him for the extra funding? What a stupid, unnecessary question. The answer is simple. I'm not used to being accountable to anyone and I don't trust him when it comes to anything beyond sex. So, damn right, it's better to ask forgiveness than permission.

Punishment, I can handle. Denial, not so much.

I work through my chores as quickly as I can, no easy task with my pussy clamped open and trying to hold in these infernal vibrating balls *and* stave off the near constant threat of orgasm.

Duncan looks up from his monitor as I knock on his office door.

"Have you fulfilled your obligations for the day?"

"Yes, Sir."

"Good, good. I need a few minutes to finish up. Come here and kneel under my desk. If you can make me come before I'm done working, your punishment will be over at seven, and you may have the rest of the evening to yourself. However, if you do not make me come before I'm done, your punishment will continue through until midnight tomorrow."

Confidently, I take my place beneath his desk, between his spread legs and pull his erection from his trousers.

As I take him into my mouth, the devil vibrator flares to life, bouncing off my G-spot with an intensity I had no idea it was capable of, and it's mere moments before I'm fighting off an orgasm.

"You are not to come, Charlotte. There will be dire consequences if you do."

Clearly the diabolical bastard had no intention of playing fair.

NINETEEN

Charlotte

One week later

"BEDROOM. Now," Duncan's voice booms through the house the moment he walks through the door.

God help me, I head straight there. Not only because His Royal Asshole demanded it. But because I need everything he'll do to me. The kinky sex is the one thing in this marriage that works.

I strip and bend over the foot of the bed, legs spread wide, my arms tucked beneath me, my hands covering my face to hide my shame.

Yes, I'm deeply ashamed. The type of sex I enjoy. The state of my marriage.

"Charlotte." Duncan's tone is full of censure and I

scramble to figure out what's got him agitated. "Up and kneel on the bed."

"Yes, Sir," I reply as I quickly turn over and reposition myself.

"There is sheep-shit all over the back seat of your car. Would you care to explain?"

Damn it. "I'm sorry. I got an emergency call about two ewes while I was out that was on my way home, and it seemed ridiculous to come back for the Land Rover and trailer and drive almost all the way back to town when I could just pop them into the back of the car. I meant to clean it once I got the ewes settled, but then I got distracted and forgot."

"Over and above the mess they made of the car, Charlotte, what you did was dangerous. Sheep are stupid, skittish creatures. Anything or nothing could have made them jump into the front of the car and make you lose control. What in the hell were you thinking?"

"I didn't know you cared." The words are snarky, but some little piece of my heart flutters at the very idea that he might feel something more for me than a skin canvas to mark and a set of warm, wet holes to bury his cock. That I might actually matter to him.

"You could have crashed and hurt or even killed someone. The tabloids would have had a field day, and—"

That little flutter I felt skips and dies, and I stop listening. I don't matter to him at all. He wasn't even concerned about the possibility of my body being unavailable for his pleasure, let alone my wellbeing in general. Just that I could have caused a scandal. Which I promised not to do when I agreed to marry him. I squash my disappointment and accept that love was not part of the bargain, no matter what our marriage vows said.

"Charlotte."

I look up to see Duncan frowning at me. And I just don't care. "Yes, Sir?"

"Back in position."

I flip back onto my stomach with my legs spread wide and my feet flat on the floor, ready to take whatever he gives me.

The jangle of his buckle is immediately followed by the whisper of the well-worn brown leather slipping through the belt loops.

"Fifteen for dangerous driving, and five for not cleaning up the mess. Count."

There's no warmup. There never is when he's punishing me. Thankfully, for the sake of my ass, it doesn't happen often.

The first stroke takes my breath away. He's held nothing back and it takes a few seconds to clear my head. "One, Sir."

Each strike of his belt lands in a different spot and by the time he's finished, my entire ass and upper thighs are on fire.

"Nineteen, Sir," I sob. One more. I can do this.

The last shot lands between my legs like a lightning strike to my pussy. The white-hot pain flares behind my eyes like a supernova in the night sky and I scream deep into the mattress.

"Do I need to start from the beginning, Charlotte?"

"Twenty, Sir," I force out between panicked breaths.

Dropping his belt on the mattress, thrusts his cock deep inside and I can't hold back the moan. I press my hands tighter against my face because I shouldn't be turned on by this. I shouldn't get off on this. I—

"Charlotte, enough. We like what we like. And fortunately for us, most of our likes complement each other."

He slams his body hard against mine, filling me, the tip of his cock banging the deepest part of me.

And that actually sums up our marriage. He bangs away at the deepest part of me while I don't even scratch his surface.

TWENTY

Duncan

Just as I'm about to come, I pull out and jack off until I spurt over her back. "Stay like that until it dries. Then you may get dressed and continue with whatever you have planned for your day. You may not wash it off until I tell you. It's to be a reminder that when my wife drives dangerously, she does not deserve my come inside her."

"Yes, Sir," she whispers as I turn to leave.

I'm still livid that she'd taken a chance like that.

I get why she did it. But safety must always come ahead of everything else.

And speaking of safety...

I pull out my phone and hit two. My bodyguard used to be number one, but Charlotte holds that spot. Has done since she agreed to my proposal.

"Craig, why the fuck was my wife out in the car without protection?"

"She was what?" he roars.

"Charlotte went to town, and then picked up a couple of sheep in the car on her way home. Where was her bodyguard?"

"I don't know, but I sure as hell am about to find out. I'll get back to you as soon as possible."

"I'll be in my office."

Fifteen minutes later, Craig knocks on my door.

"Well?" I ask.

"She told Ailsa that she wasn't going anywhere today, and she could stand down. If you want me to find a replacement, I'm happy to do so, but after this stunt, I expect Her Grace will have a harder time giving Ailsa the slip than she would someone new."

He's right. It makes more sense to maintain the status quo. And clearly, my wife needs to learn a very hard lesson.

"Wait here. I'll be back in a few minutes," I tell him as I go in search of my disobedient wife.

I start with the bedroom, and bite back an annoyed smirk as I walk in on her admiring her ass in the mirror. The marks from that punishment were supposed to be a disincentive, not a reward.

"Charlotte."

She looks over at me, guilt and shame written all over her face.

"Yes, Sir?"

"Where was Ailsa today?" I ask, purposely keep my voice quiet to keep the anger from seeping through.

"Oh, I...well...I gave her the day off."

"How, exactly, did you give her the day off? What did you say to her?"

"I told her I wasn't going anywhere today."

"And was that the truth?"

"No. I just wanted to have some space. Some breathing room to run some errands and just be me."

"That ceased to be an option the moment you agreed to marry me. What you did was foolhardy, and we can't risk you doing anything like that again. We may be a long way down the line of succession, but we still hold some value to those who might try for leverage of some sort. And on top of that, you put Ailsa's job on the line."

It's that last part that hits the mark.

"I didn't think—"

"No, you didn't."

"Did Craig fire her?"

"No. But only because we both agreed that it will be harder for you to fool Ailsa again than someone new."

Relief flits across her face, but I don't allow it to linger.

"You, however, will be punished on her behalf in addition to what you've earned for yourself. And let me be clear, Charlotte, anytime your behaviour has a negative impact on our staff, *you* alone will pay the penalty. Am I clear?"

"Yes, Sir."

"You will present in the dungeon ready for punishment by eight."

"Yes, Sir." The tremor in her voice makes me want to fuck her throat, but I have punishment to plan.

"And, Charlotte. You may not bathe."

"Yes, Sir."

TWENTY-ONE

Charlotte

"We're expected at the palace this evening," Duncan informs me over breakfast.

"What for?"

"Some function or other. I don't really know. Just that we're expected and it's formal."

"Duncan, why are you only telling me this now?"

"Because the reminder just popped up on my mobile."

"How long have you known about this?"

"Oh, I don't know. I don't pay attention to these kinds of things until I absolutely must."

I make a mental note to ask his assistant to let me know about invitations as they arrive. "I'm afraid you'll have to attend without me."

"I beg your pardon?"

"There is no way I am going to a formal function of

any sort on less than one week's notice, let alone less than twelve hours. I already have my day planned, and it does not include frantic dress shopping and hours having my hair done."

"We have a contract that says you will attend official functions."

"And I suppose I should have added a condition that I'm given ample notice?"

"*Caveat emptor* and all that."

"Fuck you, Duncan. I am not going."

"You will. The question is whether you'll be able to sit down comfortably or not."

"Duncan, please. I don't have anything to wear, and you're really being unreasonable to expect me to be able to do this and not be an embarrassment with absolutely no notice. It's fine and dandy for you. Everything you need is sitting in your wardrobe. A quick shower, drag a comb through your hair, throw on whatever tux or uniform the occasion calls for, and you're done. I, on the other hand, am expected to appear with my hair perfectly coiffed wearing a virgin designer dress because I'm sure it would be offensive to the guest of honour were I to attend wearing a dress I'd worn for some other dignitary."

"Are you quite finished?"

"I am not going."

"You are, except now you'll be going with a caned ass and tits. Playroom. Now."

"Duncan—"

"Do not push me on this, Charlotte. Because starting

right now, every refusal you give me will result in additional consequences."

"Please."

"Tomorrow morning, you can now look forward to a repeat of the caning you are about to receive. Would you like to continue, or would you like to march your ass to the playroom and take your punishment like a good girl?"

Sulking, I get up from the table and trudge my way to the playroom and wait.

When Duncan arrives, he's carrying a dress bag, which he hangs on the back of the door.

"Strip. You should already be naked, but I'll accept that I hadn't made my expectations clear. When you're done, I want you standing below the chains and facing the door. I want nothing hidden from me."

A few minutes later, my wrists are sporting suspension cuffs and attached to chains above my head, while my ankles are spread a bit wider than my shoulders and the cuffs are attached to the floor.

When Duncan is finished trussing me up, he goes to the door and unzips the garment bag. My stomach drops to the floor when he pulls out a stunning evening gown. "You made a commitment to not bring shame to our family. You should have trusted me. Trusted that I would never set you up for failure."

"I'm sorry."

"I realise I should have been up front about having your back on this. But blast it all, Charlotte, you promised to obey me. In front of God, friends, and family, you vowed to obey me, and you broke that vow. And for that, you will be punished."

"Yes, Sir."

"You will keep your eyes on that dress until I am done. You may scream as much as you need, but you will not come, and you will not speak except for your safeword. And on that subject, for punishments, I will only accept yellow as your safeword. I will stop immediately, and we will assess the situation. It will not reprieve you of your punishment, but it may delay the rest of it, if necessary. Understood?"

Short of him nailing me somewhere dangerous with the cane or me suddenly getting very ill, the chances of him getting me to a point where I'll need a safeword of any kind is slim to none. For all the asshole he is as a person, and all the evil he is as a Dom, he's exceptionally good at playing right up to my limit without crossing it. So, there's really only one answer.

"Yes, Sir."

"Ten on your ass and thighs, five on each breast."

He's lays out the ten strokes on my ass and thighs with speed and precision. They're also the hardest strokes he's ever given me, and I'm sure my screams reflect that.

"Good girl. Breasts, and then we'll be done. For today."

I groan. I'd almost forgotten that I have this to look forward to again tomorrow.

He uses a different cane on my breasts. It's shorter, but whippier than the other. He supports my left breast from beneath as he lays five evenly spaced stripes, then does the same with my right.

I scream through the whole ordeal because it's the only outlet I have for the pain. Every stroke yanks me back from any chance of reaching subspace.

"That's my good girl. I went easy on you this time because it's your first real punishment as my wife. But make no mistake, if you disobey me again, you will think this caning was like being tickled with a feather."

He releases my arms and legs, but he doesn't kiss me.

And that hurts worse than any strike of the cane.

TWENTY-TWO

Duncan

I grab Charlotte's dress off the back of the playroom door on our way to our bedroom. "Don't bother putting your clothes back on just yet. I'm not done with you. I want you bent over the end of our bed, legs spread wide." I give her bum a quick smack. "And don't dawdle."

She hurries along, and I enjoy the view of her stripes as I follow along behind.

I was a bit of a shit, and I probably shouldn't have tested her trust in me like that, but she truly thought I'd set her up for failure. Even though I've never given her a reason to think I would. She should know me better than that. That she doesn't? That fucking stings.

As soon as she's bent over the bed, I stand behind her, drop my trousers, and plunge into her. Reaching around, I squeeze her sore breasts, making her suck air and groan.

"Nothing for you today, love. Or tomorrow. If you're

a very good girl, I might let you swallow my come. But only if you're a good girl."

I fuck her hard and fast until I come deep inside her. I swear, one of the very best parts about being married is no more fucking condoms. I can fill her up with my semen wherever and whenever I like, risk free.

"Go get cleaned up and take care of whatever you need to get done today. I've got someone coming to do your hair at one. We're to be there at five for a private dinner with my parents."

She groans into the mattress, but I let it go. I don't want to have dinner with my parents any more than she does. But for now, we need to dance to their tune. At least until they're convinced I've turned myself around.

I have. Mostly. I now restrict my sexcapades to my wife in the privacy of our home.

Charlotte gets off the bed and flees to the en suite. Seconds later, I hear the shower start followed by a small screech, which makes me smile, and want to do more bad things to my wife.

She lets out another little shriek when I join her in the shower. "Hey—"

I shut her down with a kiss and squeeze her ass hard with both hands. She squeals into my mouth, making my cock begin to stiffen.

Pulling away, I grab her hair and push her to her knees. "Show me what a good girl you are, and I'll let you swallow my come."

She opens her mouth and I press my way in. As I hit the back of her throat, I trigger her gag reflex, making her lurch. That throat spasm is all it takes to get my cock fully hard. "Take it all for me, love. I want to fuck your tight little throat."

She pushes her way down my cock, and I help her the rest of the way. "That's right, fuck me with your throat. Be a good girl and make me come."

With my fingers tangled in her hair, I control everything—depth, speed, thrust and it's not long before I'm on the cusp of another orgasm.

"Swallow, Charlotte, there's a good girl."

By the time I'm done and help her back to feet, she's nearly caught her breath. "Did you enjoy that?"

"Yes, thank you Sir."

"You were a good girl, but you still have to take your punishment in the morning."

"I know, Sir."

I wash her body, taking special care to squeeze the places she's been caned, loving the little squeaks of complaint that escape as I do.

When we're done, I dry her body, then my own.

Yes, I'm an asshole, but I do cherish her.

At one, the hairdresser arrives, but Charlotte is nowhere in the house, and I'm immediately embarrassed at her rudeness and pissed the fuck off at her blatant disobedience. Clearly, today's lesson didn't stick.

I storm out to the barn where Darren is still cleaning kennels. "Have you seen my wife?"

"No, sir. She went out on Maisie around ten." He looks up at the clock on the wall. "She should be back by now. She said she was only going for a short ride on the grounds to clear her head. She took Kevin with her."

Damn it. The grounds are quite extensive, and she could be just about anywhere. I'm still trying to decide how best to proceed, when a sorry-looking trio comes ambling through the east paddock.

Charlotte is limping and protecting her right side as she leads Maisie. Kevin is far too somber, and I run to meet them.

"What happened?"

"I took a bit of a tumble."

"What?"

"It looks like the stitching on the girth strap failed somehow. One minute, we're cantering along, happy as can be, the next, Maisie takes offence at something and shies away, I'm on my side on the ground, the saddle a few feet away, and Maisie comes trotting back looking very confused. It was all I could do to lift the saddle back on her. With the girth compromised, walking home was my only option. I'm dreadfully sorry I'm late. I tried to get back in time. I only meant to ride for an hour."

I take a quick look at the saddle, and I'm concerned. Either Charlotte has let her tack fall into a dangerous state of disrepair—which I highly doubt—or it may have been tampered with. I don't like either possibility, but I prefer the former. I make a mental note to get someone more knowledgeable to look at it once I've got Charlotte settled.

"Let's get you seen to first, and then we'll deal with everything else, okay?"

"Okay."

Grabbing the saddle, I turn to face Darren. "Can you please take care of Maisie?"

"Of course, sir. Would you like me to deal with the saddle, too?"

"No, thank you. I want to take care of it personally."

"Yes, sir."

I don't know where I can touch Charlotte, so I don't, for fear of causing her more pain or damage. Instead, I call Craig as we walk back to the Dower House. "Charlotte has taken a fall from her horse. Can you please meet us at the house to give her a quick check over to see whether I should be taking her to the hospital?"

"I'll be right there."

I'm partway through undressing Charlotte in our bedroom when Craig arrives.

He immediately averts his eyes and comes to a screeching halt in the doorway.

"I'm sorry, I wasn't—"

"It's okay, Craig," Charlotte tells him. "As far as we're concerned, you're in doctor mode."

"But I am not a doctor."

"Close enough. Please come and tell your boss that I'm just fine and there's nothing to worry about, would you?"

"She's babying her right side, I'm concerned something might be broken."

"She can leave her bra and panties on. Now let me have a look."

Thirty minutes later, Craig is finished checking Charlotte over. "Looks like she's banged up a bit. No obvious signs of a break anywhere. She'll need X-rays to tell for sure. But if she's not in too much pain, those can wait until morning."

"Tell him I'm fine to go to this thing this evening."

There's a determined look in Charlotte's eyes, and it's clear I'd best let her have this one, even though I just want to wrap her up in cotton wool and keep her home and safe. Guilt for my anger at thinking she'd been late on purpose piles on top of my worry that she's going to overdo it because I pressed her into this in the first place.

"Fine, we'll go. But if I think it's too much for you, we'll come home directly, and don't think I won't let them know it's because of your tumble."

Actually, I'll be mentioning her fall to my parents when we arrive. They'll notice she's injured anyway, and it's best to have it all out in the open. And being horse people, themselves, they'll be understanding. And appreciative of her making the effort.

As soon as Charlotte goes to get her hair done, I pull Craig aside. "Arrange for a good saddler have a look at this, would you? The stitching failed, but I want to know whether it was poor maintenance..." I can't bring myself to say my other suspicion out loud.

"Absolutely. Anything else?"

"Is she really okay?"

"She'll be fine. I really don't think anything is broken,

and you could probably arrange to get it checked tomorrow to be sure, but let me look into kink-friendly options? Those are some impressive stripes you've left on her, and they sure as hell won't be gone tomorrow."

"Thanks, Craig. I guess I should have ensured we have a safe medical team to rely on before we—"

"What's done is done, and we'll handle it."

"Why is it, I can mark her up like that and it makes me all horny as fuck, but seeing her injuries from that fall makes me feel ill."

"Because marking her up like that is consensual. Something you have control over."

TWENTY-THREE

Charlotte

Duncan's mother is on me the moment a footman takes my wrap because my dress doesn't cover all of my injuries. "Charlotte, darling what on earth has happened?"

"I had a little riding mishap. It looks worse than it is."

"Duncan, what the devil were you thinking? Charlotte should be at home resting."

"We were expected to attend, and—"

"Stay for supper, and then take Charlotte home."

"Really, I'm fine."

"Darling, sometimes it's necessary to tough it out. Tonight is not one of those occasions."

Duncan offers his arm and we follow his parents into the family dining room where the food is laid out buffet style.

"Sit and wait here, I'll get your food for you," he says

as he pushes my chair in. A few minutes later, he returns with a plate laden with my favourites and I smile up at him. "Thank you."

I actually enjoy these intimate meals with Duncan's parents. His mother is really quite funny.

"Come love, time to go home," Duncan says when the meal is over.

"I'm truly all right to stay."

"I understand and appreciate that. But my mother has said I'm to take you home to rest, and I agree with her."

There is no point in resisting. My body is now reaching that stage where it stiffens up and really starts to hurt, and I'm grateful I won't need to slap on my stiff upper lip.

As soon as we arrive home, Duncan leads me to our bedroom and gently undresses me.

"Oh, Charlotte, I'm so sorry, love. I should have made our excuses. Climb into bed, I'll bring you something for the pain and a nice cup of tea."

"Duncan, please don't fuss. This isn't the first spill I've taken, and I highly doubt it will be the last."

"And with each spill, I will continue to fuss."

I don't know how to deal with this Duncan.

It doesn't feel real.

TWENTY-FOUR

Charlotte

It's been three weeks since my fall, and Duncan has been impossible. The X-rays he insisted upon proved nothing was broken or even cracked, and it's been well over a week since I've felt so much as a twinge. But still, he's acting like I'm more fragile than a hummingbird egg. Like I'm something to be kept behind glass and looked at as a passing fancy.

No matter how I much I needle and poke, he still won't touch me. And considering the physical is the sum total of our relationship, I'm losing the battle with loneliness.

I hadn't truly realised just how little Duncan and I interact with each other when sex isn't involved. I also hadn't realised just how much sex Duncan and I had up until my accident.

At my wit's end, I resort to drastic measures. Straight up disobedience.

Twenty minutes before I'm expected for lunch, I sneak down to the stable and tack up Maisie.

Darren comes along just as I'm tightening her girth one last time before I'm ready to mount. "I don't believe you're supposed to be riding yet."

"I'm perfectly fit to ride. Nobody knows my body better than me, Darren. Go ahead and tell my husband, but I'm going anyway."

"I'll lose my job."

"You most certainly will not. Especially if you ring him right now," I say just before I swing up into the saddle and take off hell for leather.

It's nearly two hours later when I return home. I didn't mean to be gone so long, but I'd missed the freedom.

Duncan is sitting on a chair outside the stable as Maisie and I arrive in yard. "If you're well enough for a two-hour ride, you're well enough to take care of your horse among other things. You have exactly thirty minutes to be finished and in my study."

Finally.

TWENTY-FIVE

Duncan

I know why she did it, but that doesn't make it okay. When Darren telephoned to say she'd gone out on Maisie, I just about lost my mind. Even though we'd established that the stitching on her girth strap was old and fraying, and it was an unfortunate confluence of events that resulted in her fall, and I'd had a saddler check over all her tack and do preventative maintenance, I'm still not comfortable with her out riding. Especially not alone.

I'm not surprised when her thirty minutes are up and she's not yet here. She's making damned sure she gets punished.

Okay, so perhaps I waited too long to bring things back to where they should be in our marriage. But that fall terrified the hell out of me, and I didn't want to take any risk that I could damage her further.

She makes me wait a full twenty minutes before she waltzes into my study with a cheeky smirk on her face that I will be more than happy to remove.

I make a point of looking over at the clock on the mantel, then back at Charlotte. She doesn't make the slightest effort to look chagrinned. And this pleases me. We're both on the same kinky page.

"Charlotte, did you vow to obey me?"

"Yes, Sir, I did."

"Did I forbid you from riding until I said otherwise?"

"Yes, Sir."

"And did I give you thirty minutes to be here in my study?"

"Yes, Sir."

"Yet, you went riding without permission and showed up here twenty minutes late. What does disobedience get you, Charlotte?"

"An unpleasant sitting experience that will last a great many days, for starters."

"If you recall your last lesson, love, I told you it would feel like you'd been tickled by a feather compared to what you'd have coming if you disobeyed me again."

"I do believe you did." And there's that smirk again.

She really is asking for trouble.

"Charlotte this is not a game."

"I know."

"Straight to the playroom, standing naked beneath the chains."

She practically skips out of my study. I most definitely made a tactical error, which I now need to rectify.

I give her five minutes to be ready before I enter, and I'm pleased to see she's at least obeyed me in this.

"Charlotte, I realise I babied you too much after your accident but provoking me was not appropriate. You have words, and you should have used them and trusted me. My sadism does not lean towards unpredictable pain and suffering. Better I baby you too long and make sure you are absolutely healed than risk doing damage. What if one of your injuries wasn't fully healed, and something I did made it worse? Not sexy."

"I'm sorry, Sir. I didn't think..."

"The only pain I want you feeling is what *I* choose to give you. This will be a long, hard session. As before, yellow is your only safeword, and it may delay your punishment, but that is all. You chose to deliberately provoke me in the most grievous manner. Your calculated disobedience has earned you twenty cane strokes to your ass and ten to each breast every evening before bed until I'm satisfied you have truly learned your lesson this time. In addition, every morning, I will edge you until you are on the very brink of losing your sanity. It's safe to say, you won't be coming for a very, very long time. But that is for later."

TWENTY-SIX

Charlotte

As Duncan lays out the punishment I've earned, I begin to think I may have pushed a bit too far. Perhaps I shouldn't have gilded the lily and shown up late, on top of taking off on Maisie today.

He won't take the pain beyond what I can stand. He's become an expert on just how far he can go.

The edging and no orgasms, though, that's where I'm not sure I can cope. Of course, it sounds ridiculous that being denied pleasure for an indeterminate length of time can be harder to handle than daily canings. But there we are. I'm ridiculous. And for some unknown reason, it didn't occur to me that orgasm denial would be used as a long-term punishment.

"Before we begin in earnest, it is important that I'm not distracted by this pesky erection. On your knees."

As he unbuckles his belt and unfastens his jeans, I

drop to the floor, opening my mouth wide with my tongue out ready to receive him.

Tangling the fingers of one hand in my hair, he holds my head steady as he guides his cock into my mouth with the other. "I'm going to fuck your throat raw, Charlotte. Slap my thigh three times if you have a real problem, otherwise, I'm not stopping until you've taken every drop of my come." His words make my pussy clench and throb. Being told what to expect arouses me almost as much as the acts themselves.

His cock slides along my tongue and nudges the back of my throat before he pulls back a little and presses forward again. This time, he triggers my gag reflex just enough to make my throat close against the tip of his cock.

"Take it, Charlotte," he demands as he pushes harder, farther, this time making my stomach lurch. He slides back slightly but remains lodged in my throat before he thrusts all the way in until my face is pressed against his stomach. He holds me there for a few seconds before pulling out enough for me to catch a few breaths.

"Big breath, Charlotte, I plan to be in there for a while."

I inhale as much air as I can and let some out before he drives straight in. I gag and heave against the intrusion, but he's relentless. When he's all the way in, he starts pumping his hips with quick, shallow thrusts. My lungs are just starting to burn when he pulls out enough to allow me air again, although he continues to slide his cock along my tongue.

"I love this throat, so tight. Lucky for you, I'm not going to last long. Deep breath again."

As soon as I do, he's back down my throat. His thrusts are longer and faster than before and it's not long before he uses both hands to hold my face tight to his belly, his cock pulsing in my throat until he's emptied every last drop of come into me.

"There," he says as he pulls out. "Now I can devote all my attention to your punishment. Stand with your feet a little more than shoulder-width apart."

Once I'm in position, he attaches the suspension cuffs, and raises the chains until I'm on the balls of my feet.

"I am not going to chain your ankles, but you will maintain position."

"Yes, Sir."

I watch as he pulls things from the toy cupboard. My heart sinks when he brings out the thick wooden paddle. It's not very wide, but it packs a nasty thud. And I hate it. If I thought I could get away with making it disappear, I'd have set fire to it months ago.

"As always with punishment, there will be no warmup."

The first strike of the paddle hits me square on the roundest part of my ass, almost makes me lose my footing. It's a fine balance with the heavy paddles. Stand solidly enough to keep the blows from knocking you around, but not so solidly that your muscles are completely tense. The looser the muscles, the easier it is to take whatever is being doled out.

The next strike is on my left thigh, then my ass, then my right thigh. For each thigh strike, my ass gets two. The paddling goes on forever. I'm a begging sobbing mess, and when I'm just about sure I can't take any more, it stops.

"That's an awfully angry shade of red, Charlotte." He presses a cluster of tissues to my nose. "Blow." As soon as I do, he replaces them with a fresh bunch. "Blow again."

He disposes of the tissues and comes back with the nasty whippy cane. "There's no count, Charlotte. As with the paddle, we'll be done when I'm good and ready to be done."

I wasn't sure I had any nerve endings left on my backside to react. This cane proved me wrong. Each stroke is a screaming line of fire that steals my breath. No matter how hard I cry, and scream, and beg, and plead, the fire just keeps coming, because I'm not ready to call yellow.

I'm somewhere screaming inside my head because I think my voice has given out when my heels touch the ground and my arms are lowered.

"Time to take a little break before I start work on your breasts," Duncan murmurs against my ear as he ushers me across the playroom to the bed. "On your belly, for now. I need to check if you're done or need more."

"No more, please Sir, no more."

"Not your decision, Charlotte. You got yourself here all on your own."

TWENTY-SEVEN

Duncan

It takes nearly a week for Charlotte to fully submit to her vow of obedience. Oh, she said she'd learned her lesson. Multiple times per day, most often in between chest-heaving, wracking sobs.

But words are cheap.

No, when she finally submits, she does it body and soul. And the beauty of it shakes me to my foundation.

"Charlotte." She looks up at me, her eyes still full of tears. "Come with me."

Charlotte

Taking hold of Duncan's outstretched hand, I rise and he leads me to our bedroom.

He kisses me gently before pointing across the room. "On the bed, love. On your back, legs spread."

A few moments later he's naked and slowly kissing his way up my body. I hold back my frustrated whine as he avoids kissing me where I most want it.

"Patience, love." He kisses my belly, and the tips of my nipples. God, how I want more.

He rests on his forearms as he continues kissing his way over me. Across my collar bone, up the side of my neck, and along my jaw.

Then he takes my mouth. A feather-light brush of lips, before sliding his tongue inside, tasting, teasing.

My insides quiver and I'm wet and wanting.

He strokes the back of his fingers along my cheek and this gentleness from him is...I don't even know.

His hips shift until the tip of his cock is at my entrance and he slides all the way inside me. "Charlotte, I'm so proud of you. You've earned a reward. You may come as much as you like."

He slides one hand between us and works my clit as he fucks me in long, steady strokes. After nearly a week of edging, my first orgasm comes on fast and hard. Duncan doesn't let up. He just continues on with his steady pace and I come twice more before he takes his own pleasure.

As he rolls off, he pulls me into his arms and kisses the top of my head.

"Promise you won't ever do anything to make me have to punish you like that again."

"I promise." And I mean it.

TWENTY-EIGHT

Charlotte

The envelope bearing my name is sitting on my desk when I come in from an afternoon ride. There's no stamp or postmark.

I don't think much of it. Sometimes invitations and donations are hand delivered.

Sliding my letter opener beneath the flap, I get an awful sense of foreboding. There's no reason for it. It's just there. My heart starts beating wildly, and I feel a little sick.

I reach inside with my thumb and forefinger and extract the contents.

Three photos of me. Photos I'd been assured had been destroyed. I drop them on my desk and try to get myself under control so I can think.

Who do I talk to? The number one rule is never give

in to extortion. Easy to say when it's not pictures of you, naked and bound.

I know I should go straight to Duncan. I *want* to go straight to him. But I just can't.

He doesn't know about this incident. Which means, by extension, I can't talk to Ailsa or Craig. Because they will most assuredly talk to Duncan. But I need to do something. I promised no scandals, and I need to keep that promise.

My only real hope is Winston Frobisher. He was supposed to have taken care of this, so maybe I can get this taken care of on the quiet and Duncan need never know. The thought of going behind his back makes me feel a little ill, but I don't feel like I have any other options.

Pulling out my phone, I hunt for the contact I never thought I'd need again, and I am so relieved that I wasn't foolish enough to delete it.

Before calling, I close the door to my office. This is definitely not a call I can afford to have overheard.

"Frobisher."

"Mr. Frobisher, it's Charlotte Clarence. You probably know me better as Charlotte Grey?"

"Your Grace, what can I do for you?"

"Remember when you took care of a problem for me once upon a time ago?"

"I do.

"That problem seems to have reappeared."

"I beg your pardon?"

"I received an envelope today containing three

photographs from a series I understood had been destroyed, along with a *request* for payment."

"That dirty, rotten toe-rag. Your Grace, I am truly, deeply sorry for causing you anguish. I was certain this situation had been taken care of at the time. I will, of course, get on this directly and ensure it is resolved fully with the utmost discretion."

"Thank you."

"However, I will need that envelope and its contents at your earliest convenience"

"I was just going to burn them. I don't want anyone to see—"

"Your Grace, I understand. I'm afraid I've already seen them and having the evidence in my possession will strengthen my position when I confront the offending individual."

"How do I get them to you? I don't trust the post or a courier."

"Can you get to London yourself?"

"I can try. But I'll have a bodyguard, which means— wait. I could meet Tilda at a pub for lunch, and maybe you could be there and one of us could slip them to you?"

"That sounds like it could work. Ring me back when you have your plan in place."

"Thank you."

As soon as the call is disconnected, I carefully gather up the photos, return them to the envelope, and lock them in my bottom desk drawer. Then I phone Tilda.

"Hey Charlotte. It's been a while. What's up?"

"I need an emergency favour."

"Of course, what can I do?"

"Can you please call me around seven this evening with a man-crisis? One that needs me to come to the city and meet you for lunch tomorrow?"

"Babes, what's going on. This sounds serious. Are you okay?"

"Please, can you just do that for me?"

"Of course I will."

"Thank you. You're a godsend."

"Who's a godsend?" Duncan asks as he barges through the door.

My stomach clenches and I force myself to take a breath. "Do I barge into your office without knocking when your door is closed?"

"Charlotte, you don't close your door, so I found it rather worrisome to find it so. Who is a godsend?"

"Do you really want me to ruin your surprise?" It's the best I can come up with on the fly, and now I'll have to come up with a surprise for him to make the lie true.

"Oh. No, of course not. I just came to see if you would join me for lunch."

"Yes, certainly. I'll be up to the house in just a few minutes."

He looks at me a little strangely, but thankfully, he nods and leaves.

My heart pounds and my stomach churns as I delete the call history for Winston and Tilda.

I should have just told Duncan everything. He'd expect nothing less regardless of the circumstances.

Instead I've broken his trust. Even if he doesn't know it.

As requested, Tilda calls just after seven.

"Hi Tilda, how are things?"

"Oh my god, Charlotte, I'm having the man crisis of all man crises. I am truly beside myself. Is there any possibility you can come to the city and have lunch with me tomorrow?" She's so over the top, all I want to do is laugh. But this is serious, and she's showing me just how loyal a friend she is.

"I think so, just let me check with Duncan." He looks at me, eyebrow lifted in question. "Tilda needs me to come to the city for lunch tomorrow. She's having a bit of an issue."

"One you can't discuss over the phone?"

"Some issues are bigger than a phone call. Maybe it's a man thing that you can solve all your life problems with your friends over the phone, although, if memory serves, a pint at the pub tends to be more man-style. She needs me, and I just want to know if you have any compelling reason I can't go."

"No, you go. Do you think you'll be spending the night?"

"No, I don't think so, but maybe play that part by ear?"

"Okay."

The next morning, Ailsa and I depart for the city. I'm still trying to figure out exactly how I'm going to get the envelope to Winston without Ailsa seeing. She's got eagle eyes, for which I'm sure I should be grateful, but not so much today.

"Ailsa, is there any chance you'll be able to sit out of earshot today? Tilda is going to want to have privacy, and I know you're a vault, but she doesn't exactly know you, and..."

"Let's see how things look when we get there, but I expect I can figure something out that works for both of us."

"Thank you. I appreciate it."

"Your Grace?"

"Yes?"

"I don't know if you fully understand there are very few situations where anything you divulged to me would have to go further."

"I do, understand. Thank you." Except I'm fairly certain this is exactly one of the exceptions to that.

Tilda is already at the pub when we arrive, and I spot Winston sitting at a table right on the route to the ladies' toilets.

Ailsa does a quick scan of the room, then turns to me. "How about if I hang out at the bar. I can keep an eye on the room, I'm near enough to you in case something happens, but you can still have a quiet conversation with your friend."

"Perfect. Thank you."

I wait for Ailsa to settle in at the bar before I start talking. "Tell me a whole load of bullshit right now so it looks like you're giving me the sob story. Then I'll fill you in, okay?"

"So, do you want to tell me what that was about?" Ailsa asks as soon as we're both in the car.

"Tilda needed—"

"Please don't treat me like I'm a fool. I can't protect you if you shut me out. Do you honestly think I don't know who Winston Frobisher is? And I'll give you credit, you and your friend did some rather elegant sleight of hand, there, but I saw both hand-offs. Yours to Tilda, who then slipped the envelope to Frobisher on her way to the loos. We've got plenty of time for your long story before we get back to Finleigh Park, and I meant what I said earlier. There isn't much that you could tell me that I'd have to share with anyone else."

I want to tell her to drop it, but I know she won't. "There was a thing back before I ever met my husband that Winston took care of. Unfortunately, the situation wasn't as permanently handled as we'd thought, and I just made what one might consider a warranty claim."

"I'm afraid I'm going to need the details. It doesn't matter if it happened when you were three, if there is a potential scandal, we need to get ahead of it."

"That's what Winston is for."

"Regardless, I need to know what's going on so I can figure out how best to protect you."

I turn my head and stare blankly out the side window in an attempt to hide my humiliation. "I trusted someone who took compromising photographs. I'd been assured everything had been destroyed, but yesterday I received a selection of them along with a request for payment. I gave everything to Winston. And now that you know, I'm not going to delude myself that you won't be obligated to tell Craig and my husband." Because when push comes to shove, it's the person signing the paycheque who is guaranteed the loyalty.

Aisla takes a long, deep breath and lets it out slowly. "Okay, this is definitely something I can't keep just between us. But here's what I can do. I can give you half an hour to tell your husband yourself. I'll make sure it takes that long for me to give Craig my report, and I will also do my best to have him hold off as long as he can to give you both time to work things out before he goes to your husband."

For the first time since Ailsa called me out on the envelope hand-off, my chest loosens enough to breathe. However, I can't help resenting the fact that I had to negotiate for that small concession. But it could have been worse, I suppose. "Thank you, Ailsa. I appreciate you giving me an opportunity to get ahead of this with Duncan."

TWENTY-NINE

Duncan

I'm in my study buried in the financials for a company I'm thinking about buying when Charlotte bursts through the door.

"What's wrong? Is Tilda okay?" I ask as she drops to her knees on the floor next to my chair.

"I'm in so much trouble and I don't even know where to start."

"From the beginning is usually a good place."

"Duncan, I'm so sorry. I thought it was behind me. I should have—"

"Slow down and tell me what's wrong."

"I don't have much time. Ailsa said she can give me half an hour to fill you in—as long as it takes for her to tell Craig—"

"And you're wasting precious moments. Deep breath,

and then start at the very beginning. I promise I will hear you out before I will allow Craig to have his say. Okay?"

The relief on her face makes my heart squeeze a little.

"Before you and I met, before I even knew about Fetwrk, I'd discovered the kink scene. I was stupid, I made a huge mistake and trusted the wrong person entirely too much. I let him blindfold me when we played, and he took advantage of that and filmed me. Stills and video. As soon as I found out, I went straight to Winston Frobisher. I was too ashamed and embarrassed to be able to tell him exactly what had happened, but he introduced me to Mel Seymour."

I smile. It appears I owe Mel Seymour for my good fortune as far as spouses go. Also, now I know the story behind what Craig found before we married.

"Anyway, Winston had taken care of the situation and I thought nothing more about it until yesterday when I found an envelope on my desk addressed to me containing a number of the offensive photos and a demand for money. I called Winston—who was totally horrified—and we arranged to meet today so I could give him everything and he said he would take care of it."

"Why didn't you come to me?" I try to keep my voice even, despite my anger.

"I'd promised you no scandal. I was ashamed and mortified at my stupidity. I never wanted you to know that about me. It happened before I'd ever met you, and I was certain it had been dealt with. It hadn't, and I needed to fix it."

I take a deep breath and let it out slowly. "No, Charlotte, you *didn't* need to fix it. You needed to *trust* me. You should have come to me yesterday and given me the opportunity to support you in this. Instead, you assumed the worst of me."

"I'm sorry."

My phone rings, and Craig's name pops up on the display.

"Up you come," I tell Charlotte as I guide her onto my lap and pull her in tight and answer my phone.

"Craig, I don't think there's anything you can tell me that I don't already know. So, I think it's best you call Frobisher and coordinate your efforts to make this all disappear as quickly and quietly as possible."

"Yes, Sir."

Hitting the end button, I place my mobile in my pocket and cradle Charlotte as I rise from my desk.

"Let's go lie down for a while. I think we both need to just be. I need to think on your punishment. I'm angry and disappointed you didn't trust me enough to tell me what was going on, but mostly disappointed."

"I'm so sorry."

"Hush, love. It will be fine."

Charlotte falls asleep on my shoulder, and I think about everything she's told me. The first thing that's clear is she didn't make her decision out of disobedience, or even an attempt to hide it from me. Her concern was breaking her promise. And given I never expected her to be involved in any scandal—let's face it, that was always likely to be me—I'd never actually laid out the terms of the punishment. I suppose, she could reasonably have expected I'd want to sever our ties as quickly and quietly as possible.

I lean over and kiss the top of her head and she wakes up.

"I've done a lot of thinking while you were sleeping, and I've decided not to punish you. You were scared, and you made a tactical error. However, from now on, I need your promise that you'll come to me, no matter what. This could have been an absolute disaster, and I won't accept any more risks."

"I promise."

"Now, is there anything else in your past that could come back and bite us in the ass?"

"No."

"You're sure? Because I want to know about every single little thing, no matter how deeply you believe it's buried."

"No. That's truly the only thing ever."

"All right then. As soon as Craig and Frobisher have this incident done and dusted, then we'll say no more about it. Clean slate."

"Thank you."

THIRTY

Charlotte

It's nearly four in the morning, over a week later when I wake up feeling nauseated and sneak off to the main bathroom on our floor because I don't want to wake Duncan.

I remain there until there's nothing left in my stomach and return to bed.

Eventually, I fall asleep until Duncan pinches my nipples. "Wake up sleepyhead."

I'm still feeling kind of off, but not enough to say no.

He's quick this morning, but he makes sure I come, for which I'm grateful. He's become a very big fan of orgasm denial, so coming is no longer guaranteed.

"Don't forget, we have that gala this evening."

"I remembered. I do wish your parents would let up on the number of functions we are required to attend. I realise they think it will help rehabilitate your reputation, but honestly, it's becoming intrusive." In addition to the nausea last night, I've been awfully tired, and it's likely because I'm burning the candle at both ends. Working here most of the day, and at least once a week, sometimes more, expected to attend some event that eats into my down time.

"I'll arrange a meeting with them to discuss it."

"Thank you."

Shortly after breakfast, I'm nauseated again, and make a run for the bathroom where I lose everything I'd just eaten. Once I'm sure I'm not likely to embarrass myself, I go find Duncan in his study

"Duncan, I need to bow out tonight, I'm feeling decidedly under the weather."

"You were perfectly fine to fuck, not much more than an hour ago."

"I really do feel quite off."

"Considering you insisted on attending a function after taking that nasty spill off Maisie, how the hell do you expect me to believe a flimsy excuse like 'feeling under the weather? It's not like you've never lied to me before. Do you need to relearn your lesson?"

"No, Sir. I'll be ready to go on time."

The morning goes smoothly, and I'm relieved to find that either the tablets have helped with the nausea or my tummy upset has run its course. Perhaps I shouldn't have jumped the gun and tried to get out of attending tonight's function.

I take Kevin out to play with the sheep. We're just about halfway to the sheep paddock when I'm hit with the most excruciating pain. My vision starts to darken at the edges, and I can't keep myself from falling.

THIRTY-ONE

Duncan

I truly fell in love with Charlotte the day she fully submitted to me all those weeks ago, but I've been in deep denial.

It was so much easier for me to go along deluding myself that our relationship was nothing more than a merger of convenience with the added bonus of regular kinky sex.

"She's going to be fine. She's strong and stubborn," Craig says as I continue to pace the small private room where we're waiting.

"I should have—"

"What? Never had sex with her? Because let's face it, that's the only way she wouldn't be in there right now."

"Exactly. I should have kept our marriage strictly on paper."

"There's no possible way that could have been an

option. You already had encyclopaedic carnal knowledge of each other. There is no scenario on the planet where you two don't continue burning up the sheets."

He's right. Of course, he's right. The only way I could have a sexless marriage would be if I'd never fucked the woman before. And even then...

"It is my fault for not wearing condoms. I should have taken at least part of the responsibility for birth control."

"That's between you and your wife. You did discuss it, didn't you?"

"Of course we did."

"Then beating yourself up over this isn't going to do her any good. When she comes out and wakes up, she's going to need you to be there for her, not wallowing in your own self-pity."

"Fuck you, Craig."

He just laughs. And that's okay. He knows exactly how to handle me.

Seconds later, he pulls his phone from his pocket and scowls.

"What's up?" I ask.

"I know you don't need this on top of everything else, but I guess word has got out. The paps are crawling all over, trying to get access. Damn, there should have been a public statement released before they got wind of this."

"In that case, I suppose I should go speak to them."

Craig nods. "I'm no PR person, but it's better to get ahead of this as much as we can before imaginations run rampant. And maybe it's better coming directly from you."

"Let's go."

Craig escorts me to the main entrance of the hospital where I'm assaulted by a barrage of shouted questions. I stand there, tight-lipped, until it becomes clear that I won't respond. Finally, they get the message and quiet down.

"I'm here to make a very brief statement. Earlier this afternoon, my wife was rushed to hospital and diagnosed with an ectopic pregnancy. She is currently in surgery. Please respect our need for privacy at this very difficult time."

More questions are shouted, but my only focus is Charlotte and the closest I can be to her right now is inside that blasted room down the hall from the operating theatre.

"I'll arrange for updates to be made available to the press so you can put all your energy into being there to support Charlotte."

"Thank you, Craig. I know it's not part of your job."

"Protecting you is my job. Sometimes, that's more than just your physical well-being."

Once we're back in the private waiting room, he starts making calls. I ignore the substance of them. It's more background noise as I wallow in my guilt over the way I treated Charlotte this morning.

She'd told me she was feeling unwell and I'd dismissed her out of hand.

In retrospect, what I interpreted as obedience was her gathering the internal strength necessary to do as she was ordered.

She went off about her day, and I went off to attend an executive meeting. Which is why I wasn't there when she collapsed and why I didn't get a chance to apologise or tell her I love her.

I'm still lost in recriminations and regrets when the door opens.

"Your Highness?"

I turn to look at him, quickly studying his expression for any sign of what he has to tell me.

"Her Grace is out of surgery, however her condition is quite serious. Her fallopian tube ruptured and was irreparable. She lost a fair amount of blood. We're cautiously optimistic she will make a full recovery and still be able to bear children."

"Can I see her?"

"She's still in recovery. Someone will come and fetch you once she's awake."

More waiting. "Thank you."

As soon as the doctor leaves, Craig puts his hand on my shoulder. "That sounds pretty positive to me. While we're waiting, how much of that do you want to release to the press?"

"Just that she's safely out of surgery, and we're hopeful for a full recovery. The details are nobody's business but ours."

He moves away from me while he rings the press liaison, who will be losing his job once I'm not mentally paralysed with worry. There is no way I should have had to personally address the press today. All I can hope for right now is for him to not botch this, too.

A few minutes later, Craig returns to my side. "It's taken care of. I know damned well you're going to give him the sack, so I went under his head to his deputy."

"Thank you."

It's well over an hour after Charlotte got out of surgery before a nurse comes in to escort me to see her.

My heart shatters at her ashen skin. She looks over to me, her eyes filled with tears. "Duncan," she croaks.

"Hush, love." I hurry to her side and take her hand, the one that doesn't have tubes coming out of it. "Sweetheart, I am so sorry." God, where do I even start with all the reasons I have to be sorry.

"I don't think I can make it to the gala tonight."

I try to chuckle at her attempt at levity, but I don't have it in me. "Charlotte, I'm sorry I was so beastly to you. I'm sorry you lost the baby."

"Me too." I open my mouth to speak, but she squeezes my hand and gives me a hard look. "I wasn't ready to be pregnant. To be a mother. But losing that baby before I ever knew she existed—it's like retroactive love or something. And now I have this big hole in my heart."

We'd never actually discussed having children. I think I assumed we would forever be the doting favoured aunt and uncle. Spoil them rotten and send them home. No responsibility.

"I understand exactly what you mean. Charlotte, I love you. I have for quite some time, and I should never have held that back. My life without you in it would be bleak and barren and unbearable."

"You love me?"

"So very much."

"I love you, too."

"That doesn't mean you no longer have to obey me, though."

She gives me a small smile that means everything to me. "I live to obey you, Sir."

EPILOGUE

Duncan

Two years later

"I can't."

"We are so close to meeting our baby, but you need to—"

"Do *not* tell me what I need, you fucking royal pain in my ass. I've been at this for years, and I'm just too damned tired to do it anymore."

"You made a solemn vow to obey me, and you will bloody-well push, Charlotte."

My hand feels like every single bone is broken from her squeezing, but it's the tiniest price to pay for the amazing gift she's giving me.

After the ectopic pregnancy, we had a long, hard discussion about what we wanted in a family. The loss of that first baby made us both realise we would like children of our own, if we were meant to be so blessed. But we also wanted to wait until the pain was less raw, and we had settled into our new marital dynamic, which now included love.

And until we were absolutely sure we were ready to start trying for a baby, I wore a condom for added protection.

Charlotte lets out a long, loud groan and squeezes my hand harder than before as our baby's head finally appears.

"Good girl. We're nearly there."

"One big push for me, Charlotte," the doctor says from between her legs.

"Duncan, please make it all go away."

"I'd do anything for you love, and if I could, I'd have this baby for you, too. But the best I can do is be right here."

She pushes once more, and I kiss her hand, her face, her lips before the baby is placed on Charlotte's belly. "Congratulations, it's a girl."

"A girl? Are you disappointed?"

"How could I be disappointed? You made us a beautiful baby who I love every bit as much as I love you."

Many hours later, Charlotte and I take our new baby home where I promptly put them both to bed.

"I want to protest," Charlotte says, "but I'm really so very tired, I don't have the energy."

"Sleep. You've had a big day."

I recline next to her with my back against the headboard and stare at our little miracle fast asleep in my arms.

"Duncan?"

"You should be sleeping," I admonish.

"I will. I don't want to name her Victoria anymore."

"No?"

"No. She's definitely not a Victoria."

"What did you have in mind, then?"

"Dylan."

"Seriously?"

"She's not a Victoria."

I look down at our precious wee girl. "No, she is definitely not Victoria. Hmm. Dylan." I roll that around in my head for a bit. My family is rife with naming conventions, and the very idea of deviating from them will likely give my mother a fit of the vapours. "I like it. We may have to concede a family middle name or two in order to mollify my parents."

"There's nothing to say they have to be girl's names, though..."

Just one more reason I love this woman, if there's a loophole, she will find it.

THE END

ACKNOWLEDGMENTS

Susan Hayes for all the innumerable awesome ways she supports me.

Zoe York for the gorgeous cover and for always being available to help whenever I ask.

Tymber Dalton, for brainstorming and hand holding.

Vera and Nancy, for being the best eagle-eyed beta readers who catch the things I miss! You are treasures. Thank you, my lovelies.

As always, my truly lovely Dayna Hart who takes the insane jumble of words I send to her and helps me untangle them into something readable.

And finally, my husband for accepting that crazy is part of my process.

ABOUT THE AUTHOR

Surrounded by mist-covered mountains, Sadie Haller lives a quiet life with her husband and fur-babies.

Where to find Sadie
sadiehaller.com
sadie@sadiehaller.com
Follow on Bookbub

www.ingramcontent.com/pod-product-compliance
Lightning Source LLC
Chambersburg PA
CBHW010511100726
47902CB00011B/2168